TORN

DARK LEGACY, BOOK 2

NATASHA KNIGHT

Copyright © 2018 by Natasha Knight

All rights reserved.

No part of this book may be reproduced in any form or by any electronic or mechanical means, including information storage and retrieval systems, without written permission from the author, except for the use of brief quotations in a book review.

ABOUT THIS BOOK

Taking her is my right.
Breaking her, my duty.

I was always going to choose Helena. I knew it the instant I saw her.

She's different than the others. There's a darkness about her. Something wild inside her. And it calls to the beast inside me.

But she isn't what I expect. With every word and every touch, she pushes me, burrows deep under my skin, challenging the rules, upending history.

And all the while, I see how my brother watches her. He wants her, and as the rules stand, she'll become his in one year's time.

Except that I have no intention of giving her up.

Torn is the 2nd Book of the Dark Legacy Duet. If you haven't yet read Taken, you'll need to do that first. You can find it in all stores now. Click here for the links.

PROLOGUE

Helena

I can't open my eyes.

It's like a dream where you will yourself to wake, to escape, but you can't wake up, and there is no escape.

Water drips somewhere nearby, behind me maybe. The sound echoes off the walls.

The stomach-turning scent of decay permeates this place and all I can think is I'm back on the island. I must be. And in that mausoleum.

They've buried me alive in that mausoleum.

The scene changes then, taking me back to the library, to where my sisters and I stood on our blocks. Where he took his time looking us over. Took his time as he decided.

I remember his eyes, the darkness inside them.

And I feel his touch, his fingers on me, on my sex.

And I remember my arousal.

I struggle against the memory and it changes again and I see my parents.

My mother.

Much like our enemies, we Willows are a family plagued by lies and deceptions.

First, it was my parents who betrayed me. Sold me like a prize pig. Sebastian's words, not mine. But it hardly matters who spoke them.

Then, it was Sebastian.

He told me to trust him, and I did. He told me he had a way out, and I believed him.

But he's been lying all along.

And I've been a fool all along.

1

HELENA

I dream of my aunt that night.

I always thought I'd know when she died. I thought I'd feel it. But she's been gone for weeks and I haven't felt a thing.

But in my dream, she's young and beautiful. She's holding my face in her hands and they're soft, the skin no longer old, but like mine. Looking at her face is like looking in a mirror.

She was me seventy years ago. She was the Willow Girl. You could swap us out for one another, no one would know.

I am an exact replica of my aunt.

She's smiling and watching me and all I can do is cry as I try to understand. To make sense of this.

"You have to be strong now, child."

"You're gone, and I didn't even know."

"I only stayed as long as I did to give you this,

Helena." She touches the ring, turns it on my finger. The bone is smooth and cool against my skin.

"Did you kill him?" I ask. "Is it true what they said?"

"They lie," she says, turning her head a little, looking into the darkness beyond and I see the edge of something on the curve of her neck, a scar I've never seen before. "Never forget that."

"What's this?" I start, pushing the loose black sheath-like dress away.

She catches my hand to stop me.

"Look in the closet, Helena. In the floorboards."

"What?"

"The closet in the Willow Girl's room. Look. You'll understand." She touches my ring. "Remember, we have a piece of them. Let that knowledge be your power. Let it give you strength. You'll end this. You'll be the last Willow Girl."

"Am I going to die?"

She hugs me to her, cups the back of my head, and she's old again and familiar again.

Noise startles us and she looks beyond me into the dark. I wonder if she can see inside it. I can't.

"Our time is up, child. You remember I'm with you and the ghost of every Willow Girl is with you. You'll end this."

"I don't want to be one. I don't want to be a ghost."

And before I can even say goodbye, before I can

squeeze her one more time, she's gone. Vanished. And the sudden noise is loud and makes my head throb.

I try to open my eyes, but they feel like they're glued shut.

"Get up," a woman says.

She must be kicking my bed because I'm jolted.

I don't want to be one. I don't want to be a ghost.

"Ethan, get her up."

It's Lucinda. I recognize her voice.

And a moment later, an instant before I can peel my eyes open, a splash of icy water drenches me, steals my breath and has me gasping for air.

I open my eyes, rubbing my face. My head throbs and I feel like I want to puke.

When I sit up, a wave of nausea almost has me falling over.

I'm on a bed, more like a cot, in the middle of a room or what was once a room, the smell that of damp and mold, like a place closed up for too long. A place damaged by water, old and forgotten.

I count the constant drops of water as my eyes adjust to the dim light and two figures come into focus.

Lucinda stands across the room. She's wearing a long black dress, covered from neck almost to ankle.

Closer to me, holding the now empty bucket, stands Ethan. I'm grateful the light is dim because I don't want to see the look in his eyes.

"Not laughing now, are you?" he asks, and I forget what Sebastian said about the accident that damaged him because right now, Ethan Scafoni scares the crap out of me.

"Where am I?" I ask, looking around.

Along one of the four walls there's a boarded-up window and it's either nighttime or we're underground because there isn't a break in it. Not a single crack that lets in the dimmest light. On another, there's a huge, heavy wooden door.

I know we must be in some sort of basement from the smell. Dark and dank, the scent overwhelming.

"What did you do to me?" My head is throbbing and when I reach up to touch it, I realize I'm naked. "Where's Sebastian?"

"You still want him after what he did to you? How he lied to you?"

"Where is he?"

"What a stupid girl."

"Where am I, Lucinda?"

I hug my arms to myself, trying not to show my panic, shivering. It is so cold here, so opposite the heat of the sun on the island.

"You're not far from the island, don't worry. We'll see how long it takes my stepson to find you."

"You set me up. You lied to me."

"I told you I was helping myself."

"What do you want with me?"

"Not what *I* want. I made a deal with Sebastian. But I don't like his terms so I'm adjusting them."

"What do you mean? What deal?"

"Ethan, go get me my cane," she says, keeping her eyes on me.

His grin is wicked as he sets the bucket down and leaves the room, the heavy door creaking behind him.

Lucinda steps toward me.

"Sebastian claims to want to protect his brother, but he chooses you over him, so I'm going to make sure my son gets what he's owed before I comply with Sebastian's terms."

"What are you talking about? What terms?"

"I'm taking Ethan away, like he wants."

"What?"

"But he'll have his turn first. You won't beat me, Willow Girl."

Ethan returns. He hands the cane to Lucinda.

"Do you know this is one of the canes I used to discipline Sebastian?"

I don't answer but watch her as she walks a circle around the cot.

"It was easier when he was younger, but as he got older, he grew more and more defiant. His father allowed it, though, and if he wouldn't submit to me, Joshua would make him."

"You're going to get it, Willow Girl," Ethan chimes in from behind her.

I shift my eyes to him only momentarily, still following Lucinda as she runs the length of the cane through the palm of her hand.

"It wasn't until his father died that he attacked me."

"Attacked you? You beat him."

She stops, leans in toward me. "Disciplined, girl. Disciplined. Like I did your aunt."

"You're disgusting."

Her lip curls. "You want to see disgusting?" she asks.

I don't reply before she starts to undo the top buttons of her dress and turns so her back is to me. She pushes the dress off one shoulder and I gasp at the deep scars there. Like my aunt's.

"That's what Scafoni men do to their women. And you still call for him to come to your rescue."

"Sebastian didn't do that to you."

"No, he didn't. But he did take a turn." She turns to face me again, buttons her dress back up. "Now get on your hands and knees, Willow Girl."

I shake my head, glancing from the cane to Ethan. "If you hurt me, Sebastian will kill you."

"Ethan," she calls out.

Ethan steps toward us.

"Make her."

But at that, he hesitates, looks at me, then at her, confused.

"He said I can't touch her again."

Sebastian.

He's talking about Sebastian.

Lucinda looks at him, rage in her eyes. "Make her, Ethan."

He's shaking his head, fear in his eyes. "He said no. He said I can't touch her."

"And I say you can. She's yours too. You have a right. Take what's yours."

"Don't, Ethan. He'll be mad at you," I say, desperate to buy time.

But the instant I do, I feel the sharp pain of the cane across my middle. I double over, clutching my belly, the line hot to the touch.

"You stupid whore. You think you'll turn my son against me?" She strikes again, landing a stroke on my side. I turn away from her, try to protect my face, my belly, and she uses it to her advantage, laying three strokes across my shoulders, making me scream.

She fists a handful of my hair and tugs my head backward. Her face is an inch from mine when she spits her order.

"Lie down and take it or I swear I will break your back."

She pushes me forward and I don't doubt she will do what she says. I lie down on the decrepit mattress and grip the edges of the cot as she rains down stroke after stroke on my back, ass and thighs, each one harder than the last, until I'm sure I'll pass out from the pain.

I feel the warmth of piss between my legs. I've lost control of my bladder and she's still beating me, and I think I'm going to die.

God, I want to die.

I'm limp by the time she stops. My arms hang from the sides of the cot. The floor is gritty against the backs of my knuckles and I remember the angel over the mausoleum.

The Watcher.

I remember how her hands were carved into the stone, curled into the ground, not even holding on, defeated and yet watchful.

But I'm not carved from stone.

And I am only defeated.

I have nothing left.

Her shoes click as she walks across the room, and I hear her whisper, giving some order to Ethan. He comes toward me and I pull away, but can hardly move and where would I go? He stands on the side of the bed and I can feel his eyes on me and a brand-new wave of fear turns the blood in my veins to ice.

No.

Please not this.

Not this.

The beating I can take, but this?

I hear him unzip his pants.

God. This isn't happening. This can't be happening. Please God don't let him do this.

Don't let him rape me.

Please.

Please.

Please.

I wretch then, half on the cot, half off. I'm waiting to feel his hands on me, waiting for him to pull me apart.

And then I hear him. I hear his grunts. Feel the weight of his knee on the bed.

"I'm not touching you," he says.

I try to drag myself away.

"Sebastian says I'm not to touch you."

I don't watch him.

I bury my face and, after a few more minutes, I feel the first spurt of cum on my back. I hear the sounds he makes as he pumps his dick with his hand, covering me, my hair, my back, my ass, careful not to touch me, not with his knee, not with any part of himself.

When he's done, he stumbles backward. I open my eyes and look at him looking me over, taking in his handiwork.

He zips his pants and walks out the door and this time, I hear the lock turn and I lie there, in my own vomit. In my own piss. Covered in cum.

2

HELENA

I don't know how long I lie there. I fall asleep and when I wake up, I'm sore and freezing cold. I turn my head, wipe my face off. I stink of puke and piss and the smell of stale water permeates this forgotten place, and all I hear is that constant drip, drip, drip.

It will drive me insane.

My mouth is dry. I'm so thirsty.

It takes me a long time to get up, and I walk with difficulty to the door. I pull at the rusted ring to open it, but I know it's locked. I heard them lock it.

I call out once, twice, my voice small and cracking, but I hear nothing back. Nothing but water all around me.

The light bulb flickers on and off and a new panic overtakes me. To be here in the dark, in the pitch black, I can't. I can't think about that.

I walk to the boarded-up window and reach up to touch the wood, try to get my fingernails around the edges, but it's solidly in place and I know I'm underground. If this was ever a window, it's beneath the earth now.

I look around for something to pick the lock. For anything. But I find nothing. Nothing I can use to pry the door open.

Is this where I'll die? Buried alive in this forgotten place?

A chill has me hugging my arms to myself. I'm thirsty. I'm so thirsty I consider drinking from a small puddle of dirty water in a corner that's leaked in from a crack in the wall, but when I bend down to touch it, it's slimy. I wipe my hand off on the wall and return to the cot and sit. It's still wet from him or me. I can feel his stuff on me, caked and dried and disgusting.

But at least he didn't touch me. At least he was too afraid of Sebastian to touch me.

Lying down on my side, I close my eyes, tracing the risen line on my belly, not daring to touch those on my back. It hurts to even hug my arms into myself.

I think about what Sebastian said. How he watches me sleep. How he says I sleep most soundly when he wraps an arm around me, cocooning me.

I wish he were here now. I wish he'd find me now. Bust through the door and take me back to the island. Clean me up and lay me down. Lay me down in his bed and cocoon me in his arms and keep me safe.

Tears lull me to sleep. My thirst is what wakes me the next time. It's so powerful, it hurts.

My stomach aches from hunger and I wonder how long I've been in here. I wonder if I'll die down here before Sebastian finds me, if he's even looking for me. I try to sit up, but it hurts too much.

At least the light is still on.

I try to sleep, try to will my Aunt Helena to come to me in my dreams. To help me get out of here.

The ring on my finger burns.

Scafoni bone.

I want it off me. Want it gone.

In a strange panic, I sit up, wincing at the pain, and tug at it, tug and tug. But it's stuck, and it won't budge. Why did they leave it on me when they took everything else?

I lie back down and the next time I wake, it's pitch black. The light isn't flickering anymore. It's out now.

The weight of a hundred tons of earth seems to bury me and if I'm not careful, I'm going to suffocate. I hug my arms to myself and will myself to sleep because I'll go mad in this dark. I drift in and out and I don't know how long this goes on for. I don't know how long I lie here like this getting weaker and weaker, my throat burning, not sure if my eyes are open or closed because it's so dark and I'm scared. I am so scared.

I'm going to die down here. They've buried me alive.

Aunt Helena didn't answer that question when I asked it. Maybe she knows.

My eyes burn but no tears fall. None are left, and I sleep again. I go in and out of sleep, never fully waking, and I'm sure I'm dreaming when I hear it. Hear him.

"In here!"

I try to blink. Water drips. My God, that constant dripping of water. It's like the ticking of a clock, counting down to the end.

"Helena?" A deep voice calls.

I roll from my belly onto my side. My eyes feel crusty, dry. I touch my lips, they're chapped.

"Helena?" It's more urgent this time and I want to open my eyes, to call out that I'm here.

But then the door crashes, the wood splintering. I'm startled and I'd scream if I could. I'd scream as a flashlight shines in my face and I can't open my eyes. After all this dark, it's too bright.

"She's here!" It's Sebastian. "Helena?"

I can't lift my head up and I can't keep my eyes open. I want to cry but there's nothing left in me. I feel like I've dried up.

"Fuck." It's Gregory and my mind flashes back to the boat, to how the man lit a cigarette after dropping me to the boat floor. After shoving me aside with the toe of his shoe like you would a piece of trash, something you don't want to touch.

But it wasn't him. It wasn't Gregory. I know the way his hands feel. I know his scent.

And I know he wouldn't have done that to me. I know.

Don't I?

"Holy fuck," Sebastian says.

Something light as a feather touches my back, my side.

"Helena, can you hear me?" He's crouching down close to me, touching my face. I feel his fingers at my neck. He's checking my pulse. I'm that far gone.

"We need to get her out of here. Get her to a doctor."

I feel him then. I feel him lift me up. I feel his arms around me and my head rests against his chest and I cling to him, wrap myself around him with the last little bit of strength I have.

And when I open my eyes to the tiniest slits, I find Gregory watching us.

Watching me.

3

SEBASTIAN

Helena sleeps for three days. I have a doctor and a nurse on the island and I'm keeping vigil over her. She was so dehydrated that if we'd been even hours later, she wouldn't have made it.

They left her down there, underground in that forgotten level of our building.

As beautifully restored as the upper floors are, so is that space the opposite. Uninhabitable.

I didn't even know Lucinda had a key to the chamber she locked Helena in.

Her body was ice cold and she could barely open her eyes. Covered in vomit, piss and something I don't want to think about, she was left there for four days without water or food.

She was beaten without mercy and left in that pitch-black hole and every time I think about it, I want to kill Lucinda. I want to wrap my hands around her throat and squeeze until her eyes pop out of her head. I want to choke her and watch as life drains out of her.

I'm standing at the window, looking out at the water, at the dock where one boat is missing.

The sun is breaking the horizon, but I can't enjoy its beauty. I'm still anxious. And I can't get the image of Helena lying there out of my head. I can't get the feel of her wrapping her arms around me, clinging to me, clawing into me, out of my head.

"Fingers and toes accounted for."

She'd joked about that.

Well, not quite joked.

I turn back to look at her. She's lying in my bed, looking smaller than before, lost under the thick duvet, and all I can think is she could have died.

I'm an idiot for not seeing the extent of Lucinda's hate.

Going to her with my offer, wanting to spare Ethan the pain and confusion of finding out he isn't who he thinks he is, it backfired. And it could have cost Helena her life.

A movement beneath the heavy blankets has me holding my breath.

I go to her as she lets out a small groan. She's been heavily sedated up until now while they rehydrated her, fed her through a tube, dressed her wounds. I didn't want her awake to feel the pain she must have been in down in that room.

Those marks will take time to heal and I know there will be scars. Lucinda broke skin this time. Too much of it. In comparison to this beating, she'd been gentle that first time.

Helena blinks open her eyes and I exhale. She looks up at the ceiling and I see the moment recognition returns and she startles, her eyes going wide as she jerks up to a seat, wincing, clutching the duvet to her.

She looks at me for a moment, it's like she doesn't recognize me.

Like she's afraid of me.

Silence hangs heavy between us and I'm holding my breath. I think she is too. Her eyes fall to the bandage around my upper arm and I see her confusion.

"Sebastian?" she asks. Her shoulders slump and her forehead creases.

"You're safe, Helena."

She looks like she doesn't believe me. She shudders, draws her knees up and hugs the blanket closer.

"Where are they?"

"They're not here," I say, I know she means Lucinda and Ethan and I need to ask her one thing, but I don't want to. I don't know if I can take the answer. "Lucinda and Ethan aren't on the island. You're safe."

I take a step toward her but stop when her eyes go wide again.

"I'm not going to hurt you," I say, putting up my hands, refusing to wince at the pain in my shoulder.

"I know," she says. She looks around the room. My room. "How long was I in that place?"

"Four days."

I see her knuckles go white as she fists the blankets closer.

"You've been back on the island for three."

"Seven days altogether?"

I nod. "I asked the doctor to keep you sedated."

"Why?"

I go to her, sit on the edge of the bed.

"We needed to get you rehydrated and fed. And with what she did to you, Helena...I didn't want you to hurt. I'm sorry."

She watches me for a long time and I hear my own words.

"Why are you sorry?" she asks, her tone different now.

"That's a strange question."

"Is it?"

"I'm sorry I let this happen. I'm sorry I wasn't there to keep you safe from her. From them."

"My aunt is dead. You've known all along."

I take in a deep breath. I nod.

"Why did you keep it from me? Why did you let me go on and on and give me hope that you'd let me talk to her?"

I have no excuse.

"Why, Sebastian?"

"When I first found out, it was in the beginning. When you were first here." I pause, force myself to keep my gaze on hers because I am guilty. Here, I am guilty. "And I didn't care, Helena. I didn't care."

She presses the heels of her hands to her eyes, then rubs them and when she pulls them away, the skin around her eyes is wet.

"I care now," I say. "And I'm sorry. I was wrong to not tell you."

She studies me, gives an infinitesimal shake of her head and turns her attention to that strange ring which is still on her finger.

"It's bone," she says when she looks up to find me watching her turn it.

"Bone?" I ask.

"Human bone. Scafoni bone."

I peer closer, meet the empty eye sockets of the skull, feel a cold chill run along my spine.

"The missing finger," she says.

Her face is unreadable, head cocked slightly to the side, studying me.

"How do you know?" I ask.

"She told me."

"She told you?"

She nods.

"Who told you?"

"That doesn't matter right now. Lucinda told me things too."

"I'm sure she did."

"She said you chose this. She said you could have stopped it at any time. That you still can."

I don't want to answer this question, so I ask another one instead. "I need to know something, Helena."

She folds her arms across her chest and waits.

"I need to know if Ethan…if he hurt you."

"He didn't lay a finger on me. Like you said. He knew you'd be mad if he did so instead, he…" Her face crumples and again, she wipes away tears and I know she's trying hard not to cry them. "God, I need a shower."

She pushes the blankets away, but I stop her before she tries to get out of the bed.

"It's okay," I say. "You're clean. I cleaned you. It's okay, Helena."

She tugs away from me.

"It's not okay, Sebastian. She beat me and ordered him to rape me and the only thing that kept him from doing it was his fear of you. Of your wrath. And as grateful as I am for that, I don't understand why he's so afraid of you. What did you do to him? What more are you capable of?"

I stand, take a few steps away, run a hand through my hair before turning back to her.

"Why is he so scared of you?"

"It's not important. It's important he didn't touch you."

"Because only you get to dictate who touches me, right?"

"Helena—"

"Right?"

I remain silent as she rages.

"Is it true, what she said? That you can stop this, right now?"

I feel my eyes narrow, feel the tightening of my face. "It's not that simple."

She shakes her head. "Yes or no. Sounds pretty simple to me."

"Lucinda is a liar."

"And you aren't?"

I shake my head, turn away.

"You told me to trust you. And I did," she starts. "I didn't believe her when she said you were feeding me piecemeal and I just fell for it. All of it." She stops, bites her lip. "I fell for you."

I go to her, take her by the arms. "Helena—"

She shoves me away. "Don't touch me."

"Lucinda will do anything to hurt me. To hurt you. To hurt us."

"What *us*?"

"Don't let her win."

"She didn't lie—"

"You don't understand, Helena. There are things you don't know."

"What things? What things do I need to know that can redeem you? That can make me forgive you? You're the reason my aunt died. You're the reason I'm here. You're the reason every time I move, every part of me hurts. You're the reason I almost died. You. It's all you!"

"Your aunt was old." It's a stupid thing to say. I hear it myself.

"Oh!" She shoves the covers off, swings her legs off the side of the bed. Stops. Squeezes her eyes shut and grips the edge of the nightstand.

"Stay in the bed, you're too weak."

It takes her a minute, but she opens her eyes and forces herself to stand. I go to her, take hold of her arms and catch her as her knees buckle.

"Get back in the bed, Helena."

"Did you drug me? Am I drugged?"

"So your body can heal."

She drops to a seat on the edge of the bed and shrugs my hands off. "Don't touch me. I don't want your hands on me."

I hear her words but I don't let myself feel them.

She covers her face, rubs her eyes. When she looks up at me, accusation burns into me.

"You're right. She was old. And she was holding on until this reaping because somehow, she knew it would be me. And then that time came, and I never even got to say goodbye and you just kept lying to me over and over and over again."

She stands again, takes a step, stumbles.

"Get back in the bed, Helena."

"I don't want to be in your bed."

She takes another step, and this time, her legs give out. I catch her just before her knees hit the carpet.

"Get back in the goddamned bed."

I put her in it and hold her down when she tries to get up.

"Stay in the bed or I'll make you stay," I warn.

"I don't doubt you will. What else are you lying about? What else is there?"

"I almost lost you, Helena." I step backward, hearing my own words.

"You never had me, Sebastian."

Her words hit me like a fist to the gut. I watch her, rub the scruff of my jaw, see her suck back a sob.

"You're tired. You need to sleep so you can think clearly," I say.

I walk to the door.

"I want to go home."

"No."

"Let me go home. I want to go home!"

I turn to her, take a step toward her. "Home?" I snap. I don't mean my voice to come out like it does. "Home to what?"

She flinches like I've hit her.

I force myself to stop, to keep away from her before I shake her to make her understand.

"End this. You can end this!" she screams.

"Lucinda's a liar, Helena."

"You're the liar, Sebastian!"

"It's not as simple as that."

"Just let me go!"

I slam my fist into the wall. "No!"

Helena startles, her eyes go wide. I see the fear inside them.

She's afraid of me.

"Why not? Why won't you let me go? Why do you want to keep me when I don't want to be yours?"

I feel my jaw tighten. Feel the weight of cement in my gut.

"You don't mean that."

"Oh, I mean it."

"You're tired. You need to rest. I'll send the nurse in to give you a sedative."

"I don't need a fucking sedative."

She pushes the blankets away again and this time, when she gets out of the bed, I wrap an arm around her middle and force her to lie back.

"Nurse," I call out, my voice level again.

"Let me go!"

"Don't push me, Helena. Not now."

"Now's not a good time for you?"

She struggles, and I have to be careful not to hurt her.

"You need to rest. Get better. Then we'll talk."

"I'm finished talking. I want out."

"You can't have out."

"Please!"

"Don't make me tie you down."

"You're good at that, aren't you?"

"There are things you don't understand. You have to trust me—"

"Trust you?" she laughs, stops her fighting. "I don't trust you. I'll never trust you again."

The nurse steps into the room and picks up a needle from the medical tray on the dresser.

Helena looks at her, watches her prepare the injection.

She turns to me. "I just want to go home," she says to me, her voice softer, pleading, tears filling her eyes.

I sit on the edge of the bed and pull her onto my lap, cradling her tight to me.

She begins to cry, to sob.

"I'm sorry, Helena. I'm sorry this happened to you."

The nurse steps toward us.

"I don't want that," Helena says, looking at the syringe. "I don't want anything."

She's squirming on my lap, trying to free herself. My arms lock her to me, keep her close.

Helena's eyes are wide and she's shaking her head frantically as I nod to the nurse.

"I don't want anything. Please!"

"Be still now. It's just to help you sleep."

"I don't want to sleep."

But it's too late. I keep her arm still as the nurse pushes the needle in, and it works fast, the medicine. Helena's already going limp before the barrel of the syringe is fully empty.

"I don't want to sleep," she tries again.

I stand, lift her up and lay her down, tuck her in. The nurse leaves, closing the door behind her.

"You'll feel better when you wake up."

"I won't."

"You will. It's just for a little while longer," I say, brushing the hair from her face as she struggles to keep her eyes open. "Just a little while."

I walk to the door.

"Sebastian?" she calls out, stopping me.

I turn, my hand on the doorknob.

"Am I still the Willow Girl?" she's on her side, her eyes half-open.

"What else would you be?"

4
HELENA

My mouth feels like cotton. It's too warm and I push the blankets off me and turn my face but when I do, I smell him. I smell Sebastian on the pillow. On the sheets.

And I remember.

I open my eyes and it's dark. Not like in that room underground, but nighttime.

And I'm not alone.

Moonlight shines in through the window, illuminating the form leaning against the wall, watching me.

It takes me a few minutes to fully open my eyes, to focus. I pull up to a seat, but it takes effort. I feel like I'm moving in slow motion when I look to the nightstand, to the cup there.

Water. I need water.

But I'm having trouble making my arm work the

way it should, and I manage to knock the glass over, spilling the contents. I watch it roll off the nightstand, drop to the carpet soundlessly.

He moves, the shadow.

He peels himself from the wall.

I look up at him and as he comes nearer, I cringe back. When he's close enough, and his face is illuminated, I see it's Gregory.

He picks up the glass, goes into the bathroom and returns a moment later with it full. He sits on the edge of the bed and puts it to my lips and I drink, and I never take my eyes off him.

When the glass is empty, he sets it on the nightstand but remains looking at me.

"Was it you?" I ask.

"Was what me?"

"On the boat. Was it you?"

I think he narrows his eyes, but I can't be sure because it's too dark.

"You think I had some part in this?"

"Did you?"

He snorts, gets up off the bed and leans against the wall again. "If I wanted to kidnap you, you'd still be kidnapped."

I don't know if I believe him. He's so casual, so relaxed. Like he's part of this whole thing, but not. Like he's watching from the sidelines. Waiting.

"What are you doing in here?" I ask.

He shrugs a shoulder. "Not really sure, honestly."

"Where's Sebastian?"

He puts a hand on his jaw, rubs the hard line of it.

"Want me to get him for you?"

I can't tell if he's being sarcastic, but I shake my head no.

"Hm." He walks toward me, and I pull the blankets up. "I don't know what you said to him but take my advice and don't say it again."

"Why would I take your advice?"

"Because things are changing, Willow Girl."

I swallow, and I think he hears my anxiety at his warning.

"You, me and Sebastian, it's just us now. And things are changing."

I shudder at his words. At the thinly veiled threat. "I don't understand."

"Were you paying attention in the mausoleum?"

"What are you talking about?"

He snorts, smirks.

"You have a short memory." He pushes off from the wall and walks to the door. "Good night, Willow Girl. Sleep tight."

5
SEBASTIAN

I keep the nurse for another two weeks and check in on Helena sporadically in that time, giving her space. She won't talk to me. She won't even look at me. At least she's eating regularly now and able to walk, dress, and shower without help.

Gregory's sitting across from me on the patio. We're drinking whiskey and while he looks out on the dark night, I study him, my younger half-brother, his words from that night in my study, that he wants a piece of Helena, still lingering daily in my thoughts.

We share a similarity in features, dark eyes, dark hair, the cut of our jaw. He's the same height as me, built roughly the same. We think the same way too. We're both calculated.

The difference between us is that Gregory's always been last in the pecking order. And I've always been first.

I wonder if the accident with Ethan hadn't happened, if Ethan would be like Gregory.

"You're going to burn a hole in the side of my head, brother," Gregory says, turning to me.

I smile, finish my whiskey, pour another.

I don't expect him to let things go when it comes to Helena. I don't expect him to walk away from the Willow Girl tradition. From her.

And I can understand his motivation.

He pushes his glass toward me and I pour for him too, then sit back and drink a swallow of the burning liquid.

"There's a way out," he says, not looking at me. "You know the way out."

I know what he's talking about. A way out for Helena. A way for her to remain mine without breaking with tradition. With the way things have to be.

"No," I say.

He glances at me. "Suit yourself."

"She's mine."

He faces me. "I don't want to take her away. I just want a piece."

I drink another swallow, never taking my eyes from his.

"We've done it before. It's not a big fucking deal," he says.

"It's different now."

"I'm not your enemy, Sebastian."

Isn't he, though?

The air is so thick, you can cut it with a knife.

I have to be careful. With Ethan gone, Gregory will need to be managed. I always knew he'd be the bigger problem, didn't I?

"We do it my way," I finally say.

It's him who remains silent now.

"I make the rules. We do it all my way," I say.

He nods once. Holds up his glass. "Your way."

I touch my glass to his.

"What are you toasting?"

We both turn to find Helena standing in the doorway, her bare feet half inside, half outside. She's wearing a knee length pink dress that hangs off her. Even though she's been eating, she's still thinner than she was when she got here. Her nipples harden in the cool night and press against the soft cotton. She's naked underneath.

"My brother and I have reached an understanding," I say.

She studies us both, like she doesn't trust either of us.

"I'm hungry," she says instead of questioning my comment.

"That's good."

I push out the chair beside mine with my foot. It's to my left and across from Gregory.

She sits, and I signal the girl waiting nearby.

"What would you like to eat?" I ask Helena.

She looks up at the girl. "It doesn't matter. Anything is fine."

The girl looks to me, and once I give her a nod, she disappears.

"Do they have to ask permission to breathe?" Helena asks.

I smile. "You're in fine form. I'm glad to see it."

"Where are Ethan and Lucinda now?"

"They won't hurt you again."

"I asked where they are."

"If Lucinda's smart, she's deep in hiding," Gregory says.

"We'll find her," I say.

"And then what?" she asks.

"Let me worry about that."

"You won't bring them back here, will you?" she asks.

"I'll deal with them, Helena. You don't need to worry about them."

She considers, gives a half nod and turns to Gregory.

"Did you tell him what I think?" she asks him.

"About?" Gregory asks.

She faces me.

"Lucinda told me she was sending me home. She gave me that letter and said you'd been keeping it from me. She said Remy was waiting for me on the boat. She gave me my passport and told me to go, that she'd arranged a flight, which was a lie, obviously."

"Ah, she lies?" I ask.

"You all lie. It's a Scafoni family trait," she replies.

"Something we have in common with the Willows," I say.

"Just some of the Willows."

"I missed this, you know that?" I ask.

"What? Irritating me?"

I give her a grin.

"Remy obviously wasn't on the boat. It was Ethan. But there was a second man. He was the one who grabbed me. Put that rag of chloroform over my mouth." She glances at Gregory. "And I remember he lit up a cigarette just before I passed out."

"I already told you, Helena, I didn't have anything to do with this," Gregory says. "If I wanted to kidnap you, I'd kidnap you. And I know what my mother's capable of. I saw what she did to you. Believe it or not, I don't want that for you."

I look at my brother. Watch him watch her and I want to know what she's thinking. If she believes him.

If I do.

We're interrupted by the girl bringing Helena's dinner, a simple pasta dish with fresh tomatoes, olive oil and a sprinkling of parmesan cheese.

"Thank you," she says, picking up her knife and fork. She seems different, stronger somehow.

I reach over and pick up the spoon, slide the knife out of her hand and slip the spoon in its place.

She turns her gaze to our hands.

I get up to move behind her chair.

She looks cautiously up at me and I close my other hand over hers.

Gregory finishes his drink, pushes his chair back. "Excuse me."

Neither of us look up as he retreats into the house. Helena's eyes are on her plate as I move her hands, taking a forkful of spaghetti and rolling it against the spoon.

"Like this," I say, turning it, holding the forkful out to her.

She keeps her gaze on mine for a moment, and this gesture, if she accepts this, it means more than that forkful.

Helena opens her mouth and I feel a sense of relief. It's strange and not what I expect to feel.

I let her slide her hands out from beneath mine and prepare another bite for her.

She opens when I offer it, and takes the next bite too, and the one after that.

"It's enough." She says once the plate is half-eaten. She picks up her napkin and wipes her mouth. "Thank you."

I set the utensils diagonally across her plate and put my hands on her shoulders, rub them, then move them to her arms.

She doesn't pull away.

"Did you mean anything you said when we were in Verona?" she asks.

I pull her to her feet, turn her to me. I touch her cheek, cup her face. "Every word."

I kiss her.

It's soft, this tasting of her lips. Like it's our first time.

I wrap one arm around her waist and cup the back of her head with the other and I nudge her lips apart, deepen the kiss, slide my hand down to cup her ass. She's still tender there, I can tell by how she sucks in a breath.

But when I pull back, she shakes her head, wraps her hands around my neck, digging her fingernails into my shoulders.

It hurts, the place Lucinda shot me still tender. I managed to throw her aim off enough that the bullet didn't do any real damage but it will still take time to heal. It was the lamp she bashed against my head that knocked me out.

But I don't care about any of that, not right now, and I shove the half-eaten bowl of pasta aside and lift her up on the table and draw her dress up, missing the feel of her skin, the scent of her. Needing to be close to her. Inside her.

She looks down, brings her hands to my belt and unbuckles it, lets it hang there while she works to undo the buttons of my jeans. She slides one hand inside and looks back up at me.

I fist a handful of hair as she wraps her hand around my cock and I kiss her, and she squeezes my dick when I tug her head backward.

"Hard," she says against my lips, her legs wrapping around my middle as I push her backward, still kissing her, shoving my pants and briefs down with one hand.

I tug her forward so her ass is at the edge of the table and look down at her. She's shaved her pussy and I miss the triangle of hair I like to grip and tug, but I like this too. I like seeing the seam of her sex and I lean my head down and kiss it.

I missed it. Fuck, I missed her.

"Fuck me, Sebastian. Do it hard. I need you to do it hard."

I need it too. Now. Tonight. Like this.

With one hand on her thigh, I shove her leg wide, keeping hold of that fistful of hair and watching her when I thrust in to the hilt, hard like she wants it. Hard so it hurts her.

But as much as I want to pound into her, I draw back, my fingers digging into her thigh.

"Hard. Please!"

She grips the collar of my shirt, letting out a cry when I do it again.

"Helena," I grunt. She's got one hand in my hair now and is pulling. "I won't be able to stop."

I thrust again, forcing the air from her lungs.

"I don't care. I need you. I need you like this. I need us like this."

I take the wrist of the hand that's pulling at my hair and keep it on the table, lay more of my weight on her and look at her, my face an inch from hers as I fuck her. And when she reaches her mouth to kiss mine, to bite my lip, I push her backward because right now I need to look at her, to see her beneath me like this, to have her here again where no one can hurt her.

No one but me.

I close my hand around her throat at the realization.

"Why do you want it like this?" I'm still fucking her, still thrusting deep and hard. "Why?"

"Make me come. Please make me come."

"Why?"

"Because it's you and me and this is how we are. Please, Sebastian. I need this. You. Like this." She draws me closer to her, buries her face in my shoulder. "I need to forget the rest."

I grip her legs with both hands and push them wide and she's wet and tight and moaning as I fuck her deep, deeper than I've been with her before, and when I feel her spasm around me, when I hear her cry out and she's coming, I come too, my body going limp as I empty inside her, giving her everything I have, every ounce of me.

SEBASTIAN

She falls asleep easily in my bed. I watch her, curled into me, small and soft and safe.

I look at the clock, barely two in the morning.

Opposite her, I won't sleep tonight.

I never do on this night.

Pushing the covers back, I climb out of the bed, careful not to disturb her. I pull on my jeans and a sweater. The nights are cooling off, fall is fast approaching. I walk out of my bedroom, down the stairs, pick up my shoes which are by the door. I grab one set of keys and walk out of the house, heading to the water's edge.

The sand is cool beneath my bare feet and I stop to listen to the sound of water lapping against the shore.

How calm it is. How comfortably predictable. It's

always the same, no matter what. No matter the chaos on the island or in my head.

And tonight, there is chaos.

I have her back. She's safe.

After Lucinda shot me, I woke up in my bed, my arm stitched up where the bullet grazed it, a flesh wound. I wonder if I hadn't caught her wrist if she'd have hit her mark. Killed me. I wonder if that was her intent or if rage clouded her judgment.

I wonder about my meetings with Joseph Gallo. With David Vitelli. I wonder which of them turned on me. They'll need to be punished and I'll get to that.

But not tonight.

Tonight is for something else.

And Helena's back. She's asleep in my bed. She's safe.

Lucinda and Ethan are gone—for now.

I walk right up to the water, let it run over my toes. I run a hand through my hair wondering what's happened to me in the last month? Since she came into my life.

No. That's not the way to say it.

She didn't come willingly.

I stole her out of her life and forced her into mine.

She has every right to hate me, yet she doesn't. She clings to me. And I can't get her out of my head. Out from under my skin. I can't get enough of touching her, can't get close enough to her, not even when I'm buried deep inside her.

I look up at the sky, dark enough tonight that I can see stars.

It's a new moon. And it fits the day.

Black.

Today is my twenty-ninth birthday.

When the next wave reaches my ankles, it soaks the bottoms of my jeans.

I step backward. Sand sticks to my wet feet.

Time to move. Time to get off the island. Just for one night.

Gregory will take care of Helena.

I make my way to one of the two boats, climb on board, start the engine. It seems louder at night and I take one look at the house, at my dark window.

She's tucked inside, safe and sound. She'll be here when I get back.

7

HELENA

I wake up alone late the next morning. Sebastian's side of the bed is cold. It's after ten. I don't usually sleep late, I never did at home at least, but here, time is all I have.

Pushing the covers off, I get up, shower, go to my room to dress. I'm surprised when I get downstairs and don't see anyone. Both brothers must have eaten already.

I pour myself a cup of coffee, add cream and pick up a piece of toast. I take it over to the pool which sparkles like a hundred diamonds in the bright sun. I sit at the edge and let my feet hang in the cool water while I eat my toast and drink my coffee.

There's no one around, not a gardener, not any of the girls who work in the kitchen or set or clear the meals. The island is quiet. Quieter than usual. It's almost eerie and I wonder if I'm not alone.

When I finish my toast and coffee, I get up and walk around the corner and see that one of the boats is missing. I go back inside, peek into the kitchen.

Empty, not a single pot on the stove. Nothing baking. No dirty dishes in the sink waiting to be washed.

I walk to Sebastian's study and knock on the door. When there's no answer, I try the handle, but it's locked.

"Sebastian?"

Nothing.

Footsteps behind me startle me.

I know it's not Sebastian. I can tell when he enters a room.

I turn, and even though I know who it'll be, the hair on the back of my neck stands on end when I find Gregory approaching from outside. I wonder where he was. He's wearing jeans and a T-shirt but is barefoot and his hair is ruffled.

"He's gone," he says, heading to the stairs, barely looking at me.

"Gone?"

He nods. Climbs two of the steps.

"Where?"

He turns to me. "He won't be back until tomorrow."

"Tomorrow? He didn't say anything to me."

Gregory shrugs a shoulder. "Maybe he didn't

want to bust into the romantic mood of your evening."

I feel myself blush. Did he hear us? See us? He's watched before.

One corner of his mouth curves upward and he gives a short exhale as if to say it's so easy to fuck with me.

"I've got some work to do today so you're on your own," he says, before heading up the stairs and disappearing into, I guess, his room.

I glance once more at the closed study door and go upstairs to my own room, sit on the edge of the bed.

"I've got some work to do today so you're on your own."

What did he think? I'd want to hang out with him?

It takes me just a few minutes to change into a bikini, the most modest one I can find out of the dozen Sebastian ordered for me. I grab a towel and head back down.

I'll swim a few laps, clear my head. I haven't exercised since I got here and it'll be good for me.

Before heading outside, I grab a bottle of water from the refrigerator in the kitchen. I set my towel on one of the lounge chairs and twist my hair into a bun, securing it tightly so it doesn't get in my way. Then I dive in.

That first moment when I fully submerge is

always my favorite, when my head goes under and the water is cool and refreshing and the only sound I hear is that gurgling of water.

I take long strides, staying beneath the surface as long as possible, reaching the other side before I come up for air and dive back in.

This, to me, is my escape. It was the same at home, going into town to the rec center with its pool, indoors in winter and to the lake in the summer months. I wonder if I can swim in the sea here.

After too many laps to count, I break the surface, out of breath, and grab hold of the wall at the deep end. I lean my chin on my forearms and look out at the sea.

I know not to swim in the canals of Venice proper, but I must be able to swim out here. We're far enough away.

I lift myself out of the pool, water gliding off me as I swing one leg out, then the other. I stand and I turn to find my towel and freeze.

Gregory is straddling the chair next to the one where my things are, elbows on his thighs, fingers intertwined, chin resting there.

He's watching me. His hair's wet and he's changed his clothes, so I assume he's had a shower.

"You're a strong swimmer."

I have to walk by him to pick up my towel and I do, quickly, but he grabs the towel and pulls it back before I reach it.

"Can I have my towel, please?"

He lets his gaze openly run over me and I look down too. The suit is a pretty shade of deep coral and even though it's the most modest one, it's still like wearing my underwear in front of him.

He holds out the towel.

I take it, let it fall open and wrap it around me.

"Why are you here? I thought you had work to do."

He leans back, looks up at me.

"I like watching you."

I don't expect that, and I turn to go because I don't know what to do or say. But he grabs my wrist.

"Sit."

"No."

He tugs. "Sit with me."

"Let me go," I say, looking down to where he's got hold of me.

"I don't bite, Helena."

I meet his eyes. Dark, not as dark as Sebastian's though. His have specks of turquoise in them.

"Just for a minute," he says.

He must feel my resolve slip away.

I sit on the edge of the chair beside his and hug my towel close. I look stiffly ahead.

He relaxes back, puts his hands behind his head and even with my back to him, I can feel him watching me.

"I was there when he found you, you know."

I glance back at him. "I know."

"You were pretty out of it."

"I saw you there." I remember that clearly. I don't know why. "Where was it?" I ask, realizing I don't know. I never asked.

"In our building, the one where you met Joseph Gallo, the prick." His face hardens a little at the mention of the attorney's name and it makes me curious.

"But I was there. It's beautiful."

"Above ground, yes. The room where she kept you has been flooded too many times and can't even be used for storage anymore. You're lucky, actually."

"Lucky? I don't think I'm lucky."

"When it rains heavily, that room becomes a swimming pool."

I meet his eyes, which are serious. "She knew that?"

"Of course she did."

"Could I have drowned?" I shudder at the thought of being trapped as the water fills up.

"It's only flooded that badly twice."

Still. Once is all I'd need.

"I don't understand your relationships. I mean, she's your mother."

He looks off in the distance momentarily. When he turns back to me, he's still unreadable.

"Motherhood wasn't ever anything but an obligation to Lucinda. She gave my father sons, as was required of her. That's all."

"But Ethan, she loves him."

"Don't mistake control with love," he says, looking at me again. "Ethan is easily manipulated."

"What happened to him?"

"That's a story for Sebastian to tell."

I remember how afraid of Sebastian Ethan was. How he wouldn't touch me even at the risk of his mother's wrath.

"Did Sebastian hurt him?" I ask.

Gregory studies me. "You're a curious thing, Willow Girl," he says, rising to his feet.

"Did he?" I rise too. "Or is this some game, Gregory?"

He stops, and I realize it's the first time I've ever said his name.

"A manipulation?" I add.

He turns back to me, takes a step toward me. I lean away, look down, work on wrapping the towel around me.

"A manipulation?" he asks.

When I finally shift my gaze back to his, his head is cocked to the side, eyes narrowed infinitesimally.

I shrug a shoulder, clear my throat and step around him, but when I do, he captures my arm.

"Answer me, Willow Girl."

"I'm not *your* Willow Girl. I don't have to do as *you* say."

I wonder if that burns.

I want to hurt him. I don't know why, but I do.

He squeezes.

I guess he wants to hurt me too. I try to hide the fact that he does, but he sees it and smirks.

"Answer me, Willow Girl."

"You're your mother's son."

"I am that," he says casually. "But you don't know me. And you don't know my brother. Not like you think."

He releases me then and it's not me who walks away but him while a cold chill runs along my spine.

———

Gregory stays out of sight for the rest of the afternoon. I have a shower and get dressed, make my way downstairs—because I refuse to hide in my room—and walk around the island, keeping to the parts I'm allowed, until I get hungry.

I go to the kitchen to find some food and again, find it empty. For the first time since I've been here, I make my own sandwich, and eat at the small table in the kitchen. When I'm finished, I wash my dish and am going up to my room when I notice Sebastian's study door is ajar.

I smile, relieved not to have to be here alone with his brother any longer, and head to it, but when I push it open, it's empty.

Was he here? Is he back? He would have looked for me, I'm sure of it. Besides, Gregory said he wouldn't be back until tomorrow. Even if I don't like him, he has no reason to lie about that.

I go inside and close the door behind me. I can smell Sebastian in here, his aftershave just lingering on the leather and wood.

There isn't a phone on top of his desk and I wonder if there's a land line here at all or if they only use their cell phones. His desk is cleaned off apart from a laptop and a stack of papers held in place by a creepy, skull-shaped paperweight on the corner.

After glancing at the door, I open the lid of the laptop. I know it's stupid, I'm sure I'll need a password to access it, and I do. I don't bother trying to guess it, but close it instead, leaning back in the seat, stretching my legs, trying not to look at the hollowed-out eyes of the skull that seem to watch me.

My knee bumps against something rough and I pull it back. I reach under the desk, leaning down to see what it is.

Although it's dark, I can see a makeshift shelf. There's something on it and I reach in, my fingers touching cool, smooth metal. It takes me a minute to realize what it is, takes me until my hand is wrapped around the barrel of it to know.

With a gasp, I pull away, rolling the seat backward a little. I look up at the door again, take a calming breath in.

Why does he have a gun? Why does he need a gun?

I reach under again, and force myself to take hold of it, to pull it out. I set it on my lap. I've only ever seen guns on TV. It's strange to see it like this, to feel the weight of it on my lap. To know the damage it can do.

I put it back in its hiding place, unnerved by my discovery, and get up. I don't want to be in here anymore. I walk back out and close the door behind me, and I head back to my room and stay there until nine at night, when hunger and boredom draw me out.

The scent of wood burning comes from the patio and I see the back of Gregory's head. He's sitting alone watching the fire crackle as he sips his drink. There's an empty chair beside his.

I walk quietly into the kitchen and make myself my second sandwich of the day. I plan to take it back up to my room but when I go into the living room, he calls my name.

"Helena."

He doesn't turn around, but he must have heard me, as quiet as I was trying to be.

I consider ignoring him and rushing back upstairs, but I can't spend the next few years of my life in my room. I'll have to learn how to be with him. And so, I go outside and take the seat beside his. I put my plate on my lap and pick up my sandwich of cheese and lettuce, boring but what I like, and take a crunchy bite. I chew while studying the fire.

Gregory gets up, gets a second glass and pours me a whiskey.

I take another bite.

"Just you and me on the island, Helena," he says.

I glance over at him, swallow my mouthful.

"Does that scare you?" he asks.

"Should it?"

He shrugs a shoulder, takes a sip from his whiskey and turns back to the fire. "Everyone gets off the island today."

"Why? What's today? And why are you here?"

"Well, I'm here because you're here, and because today is Sebastian's birthday."

"His birthday?" I don't even know what month it is, my time is broken into days, mornings, afternoons, evenings and nights.

Gregory nods, turns to me, looks at my sandwich. "Looks delicious," he says sarcastically, raising his eyebrows.

"It is." I take a huge bite and crunch the lettuce and process what it is about this day that's so important.

It's the day his mother committed suicide.

I wonder if she chose the day on purpose. I can't

imagine it was to hurt Sebastian. My guess is she was mourning her lost son.

"Why don't you eat meat?" Gregory asks.

"Had a pet lamb once."

"Ah." He smiles, and it's a genuine one. "Mommy dearest make you eat her?"

My smile vanishes, and I think I might choke on the bite in my mouth.

"Huh. I'm right," he says.

The fire crackles and a log rolls off the carefully stacked triangle. He reaches for the poker and shoves it back into the flames.

"How did you know?" I ask.

"Just a guess, considering."

"Considering what?"

"Considering it's up to the women of the Willow family to give up their own daughters. It's a matriarchal line."

He's right.

"I never thought about it." I put the rest of my sandwich down and pick up the whiskey. I take a sip. It burns but I like the feeling of it going down. "We both have a mommy dearest I guess."

He turns to me. "If it's you, will you do it? Put your daughters on those blocks?"

I study him and I think this is the first time I'm seeing the genuine man behind the arrogant, asshole façade.

"If it were you, would you have done it? Taken one of us?" I counter his question.

He glances away, takes a minute before turning back to me to answer. "I don't know. Yes. Probably."

"No. I wouldn't," I say without a single doubt.

"Not even if it came down to that or losing everything? Your family would be wiped out."

"Financially. Wiped out financially."

"For sure, but think about it. Say it were Ethan. Say he were first born. If your mother refused, do you think Lucinda would stand back and let it be? Not make the payment, take back the Willow house and que sera sera?" He leans in toward me. "Or do you think she'd be more vicious than that?"

I shudder at the thought.

"I won't do it to my daughters."

If I even have any.

I shove that thought away.

"I guess we'll see when the time comes," he says, leaning back in his chair and shifting his gaze back to the fire.

"Why do you stay here? I mean, here you're in the shadow of your brothers. You're young, educated I think?"

He nods, eyes still on the fire.

"You have money. Why don't you leave. Do something. Anything. Do what you want."

He turns to me. "How do you know this isn't what I want?"

"You mean taking your turn with an unwilling Willow Girl?"

"I'm not sure she's so unwilling."

I swallow, feel something in my belly, something unsettling.

And when he next speaks, his voice carries a tone of triumph.

"There's something heady about owning a person, Helena. Someone like you."

I search his eyes, try to understand him. He's more straightforward than I expect. But I know he likes to fuck with me too and I know it's easy for him.

"I watch you," he continues. "Watch you with him. Watch your face. I see how you look at my brother even as he is your jailer. I watch how he keeps you, too," he pauses, takes a breath in, eyes never leaving mine. "And you know what? I want it too."

I shudder at his words and I don't know what to say. Don't know if I should get up and run and lock myself in Sebastian's room. Don't know if I should tell him he's sick. Because I don't think he's just fucking with me, not right now.

"Are you jealous of your brother?"

He shakes his head. "Not jealous. I don't begrudge him. I just want a piece of it."

My mind wanders to Alexa 2.0 and Sebastian's birthday cake analogy.

"Like birthday cake?" I don't know why I say it.

Gregory smiles wide. "If only it were as simple as birthday cake, Helena."

He finishes his drink and gets up.

"The fire will die out on its own. Sit as long as you like. I'm going upstairs."

He doesn't wait for me to say anything and I'm not sure what I would say. What I want to say. Not many people are honest like that. And I'm surprised at myself when I'm left wanting more.

8

HELENA

Ever since those days in that dark room, when I sleep alone, I sleep with the lights on. And I don't sleep well. It's like I wake up every hour or so to make sure I'm not back in that place.

When I'm in Sebastian's bed, it's a little easier, but not the same as being in his arms.

"Helena."

I stir.

"Helena, wake up."

Someone's shaking me.

"Wake up."

I blink my eyes open, squint against the light.

It's Gregory.

He's standing over the bed.

"What is it?" I sit up, look down to pull the

blanket up over the T-shirt I'm wearing. Sebastian's shirt. "What time is it?"

"Four A.M."

I rub my face, look past him to the windows but the curtains are drawn, and I can't see out.

"We need to go."

"What? Where?"

"It's Sebastian."

I'm suddenly alert. "What's happened?"

"He's in bad shape. I don't want to leave you alone on the island. I promised I wouldn't."

"Promised?"

"Promised my brother. Get dressed. Hurry."

He pushes the covers off, eyes falling to the shirt I'm wearing, to my bare legs.

I remember when he put his shirt on me that time. I remember what Sebastian said. That he didn't want his brother's scent on me.

I get to my feet, stumble to my room and put on a pair of jeans and sweater that are still slung over the arm of the chaise. I brush my teeth quickly and pull a brush through my hair and when I'm done, Gregory is waiting for me impatiently at the door.

He lets me exit first and we head down the stairs. Once we're outside, I practically have to jog to keep up with his long, urgent strides.

When he leads me to the boat, I stop, remembering the last time.

I look up at him and he must see what I'm thinking.

"I'm not going to hurt you, Helena. The alternative is staying here alone. I can't let you do that."

"Where are we going?"

"One of the casinos. He takes a room there, gambles, drinks. Gallo happened to be there. He just called me, thinks it's a good idea to go get him.

"Joseph Gallo?"

He nods. "Let's go. I'll tell you more on the way. I don't want to leave my brother there like that."

I let him help me on the boat and a moment later, we're speeding ahead and I'm hugging my arms around myself. At our speed, the air is icy on the water.

"You don't like Joseph Gallo."

"No. He's as slithery as a snake."

"Why does Sebastian trust him?"

"He doesn't."

"But why did he have me...why did we go there to sign that ridiculous book?"

"Things have to be done a certain way with the Willow Girl. There are rules."

"Rules?"

"Everything is connected. Linked to the inheritance."

"What do you mean?"

"It's complicated."

I scratch my head, try to understand. I have so many questions, but he's not going to answer them.

The lights of Venice proper come into view fifteen minutes later. The city is still buzzing this late at night and Gregory slows the boat as we approach one of the ancient buildings on the Grand Canal.

He pulls up expertly to the stairs that disappear into the water. Tall gates stand open and when the two formally dressed men holding lanterns recognize Gregory, they smile and welcome him.

He hands the keys over to one of the men and climbs off.

"Be careful, stairs can be slippery," he says, holding out his hand.

I look at it. The palm is up, offered to me.

I meet his gaze and, after a moment, I put my hand in his, and he helps me out, and I know the instant we're inside that they only allowed us in because they know Gregory because we're the only two dressed like we are.

The casino is larger inside than it appears on the outside and this isn't like anything I've seen before.

Soft music plays in the background and waiters walk around dressed like the two outside carrying trays of drinks to the elegantly dressed men and women at the tables.

I see Joseph Gallo at the same time Gregory does. He's at a poker table where a group has gathered to watch the game. He gives Gregory a nod of greeting, meets my gaze for an instant then steps aside to let us see Sebastian.

Sebastian's wearing a tuxedo. It's stretched so tight over the thick muscles of his arms that I wonder how it contains him, how the stitches don't rip right apart.

He's engrossed in the game and in his hand is a tumbler of whiskey. From here I can see the half-empty bottle beside him as he signals for the dealer to give him another card.

Gallo heads toward us, whispers in Gregory's ear.

Gregory asks a question in Italian, and after Gallo answers, he hands him a key card. Gregory takes my arm and we walk to Sebastian.

I don't play poker but from the burst of angry talk that erupts from Sebastian when another player lays down his cards, I know he just lost.

Gregory puts a hand on Sebastian's shoulder.

"Brother," he says.

Sebastian turns around but before he sees Gregory, his eyes land on me.

He's surprised, then pleased, then, when his gaze falls to where Gregory is holding onto me, angry.

"Helena." His voice is husky, and he half stands but has to grab the edge of the table to steady himself.

Gregory puts pressure on his shoulder and Sebastian winces, sucks in a breath.

I remember the bandage I saw on his arm when I first woke. I never asked him about it.

"My brother's done here," Gregory tells the dealer.

"I'm not done," Sebastian says to the dealer, but his eyes are locked on me.

Gregory ignores him, releases me to collect the chips still on the table.

"Let's go," Gregory says.

"I said I'm not done," Sebastian says, this time, turning to face Gregory as he rises to his full height.

Unsteady as he is, he's something to see. The two of them together, nose to nose, are something to see.

I take a step back and Gregory must have the instincts of a cheetah because he reaches out to grab hold of me again.

Sebastian's instincts are dulled by the alcohol, but he follows the movement with his eyes, then drags them back to meet Gregory's and for a moment, I'm sure there will be a fight. A battle between these two Goliaths.

Gregory must know this though, because he pulls me forward.

"Take her," he says.

Sebastian almost grunts, and when the pressure of Gregory's hand is removed from my left arm, Sebastian's replaces it on my right. His eyes, though, never leave his brother's.

Gregory takes the key out of his pocket and looks at both sides.

"Which floor?" he asks, walking ahead of us to the elevator and pushing the button to call it before the attendant has a chance to.

"Why don't we take him back to the island?" I ask as the elevator doors open and I see our reflection in the mirror mounted on the back wall, me, small and out of place between them, these tall and broad and beautiful men with their chiseled jaws and dark hair and darker eyes.

The aggression coming off them is so palpable, it almost crackles.

"Because I don't want to fish my drunk brother out of the canal, do I, brother?" he asks, leaning into Sebastian's face.

"Fuck you, Greg," Sebastian says.

Gregory shakes his head and turns to the man smiling awkwardly inside the elevator. "Get the fuck out," he says, practically tugging the man out. "We can push our own fucking button," he mutters this part under his breath. "Floor?" he asks Sebastian.

"Four." Sebastian turns to look at me when we get in, then turns back to his brother. "What are you doing here?" he asks. "Why is she here?"

"You didn't want me to leave her alone on the island, remember?"

"I don't need a babysitter—" I start.

"Why are you here?" Sebastian asks Gregory again.

"Because Gallo mentioned things had gotten out of hand."

"Gallo can go fuck himself."

"What did he do?" I ask Gregory.

"I'm right here," Sebastian says, leaning in close. "You ask me. Not him."

I look up at Sebastian. "You're hurting my arm."

He shifts his gaze to it, nods, releases me.

"What did you do?" I ask him.

The doors open and Sebastian stalks off muttering something.

We follow him and watch as he searches his pockets for what I assume is his key.

"He started a fight. The other guy was removed only because they know us here."

"A fight? Why?"

"Because this night fucks with him."

Gregory shoves ahead of Sebastian and slides the key card into the slot on the door. The lock clicks, and a light flashes green. He opens the door and we enter.

Sebastian immediately takes off the jacket of his tuxedo and tosses it on the bed. He removes the bow tie and undoes the top buttons and those at his wrists, then pulls the shirt off over his head. He rubs the spot on his arm that Gregory was squeezing, rotates his shoulder once, twice. I have a closer look and see the dozen or so angry looking stitches.

"What happened?" I reach out to touch one.

He looks at me. "Nothing."

He walks away, goes into the bathroom. I hear water go on.

"What happened?" I ask Gregory.

"The night you were taken, Lucinda shot him."

"What?"

"He's fine. We need to deal with this right now."

Gregory picks up the phone, orders coffee sent up to the room.

I walk toward the bathroom, but Sebastian comes out before I go in after him. He's wiping his face with a towel he discards a moment later.

He stops to look me over and looks a little more sober, although still not sober enough.

I look back at him, and he's different tonight. Like he's chasing away some demon and I'm not sure he's winning.

Before I can speak, he turns to Gregory, stalks toward him. "Why did you bring her here?"

"I already answered that."

"Did you tell her too?"

Gregory doesn't look at me and for a moment, I wonder if he'll tell Sebastian that I was in the mausoleum or if he'll keep that secret. And I realize I'm a little afraid that he will tell because tonight isn't the night I want to deal with an angry Sebastian.

A knock on the door saves us, though, and Gregory shoves past Sebastian to open it. He signs the check and takes the tray of silver service coffee.

Sebastian sits on one of the two armchairs and takes the coffee Gregory gives him. He looks at me as he drinks, and I sink to a seat on the edge of the bed. I decline the coffee Gregory offers me.

"You can go," he tells Gregory, never taking his eyes from me, setting his empty cup down moments later.

"I'm not going anywhere."

Sebastian shifts his gaze to his brother, then, after a long, calculated minute, back to me.

"Come here, Helena."

I get up, go to him. He spreads his knees and points for me to stand between them.

"Get undressed."

My heartbeat picks up and I look back to Gregory, who's leaning against the wall, watching. His arms are folded across his chest and his gaze is intense on his brother.

"No," I say to Sebastian. "Not in front of your brother."

"My brother wants his own Willow Girl. Did you know that?"

He leans back, tilting the chair a little.

"And he's got his eye on mine."

I glance back at Gregory who hasn't moved.

"Now get undressed," Sebastian says.

I turn back to him. "Sebastian—"

He slaps the flat of his hand on the table, making me and the coffee cup jump.

"Now, Helena!"

I look back once more as my hands tremble toward the hem of my sweater.

"Eyes on me. You don't need to look at him."

I swallow and do as he says. I pull my sweater over my head.

Sebastian nods and I toss it on the floor and slip off my shoes as I undo my jeans. I push them down and step out and set them aside too so I'm standing in black bra and matching panties.

"I don't think—"

"You're not here to think. Off. Everything off."

It takes two tries when I reach back to undo my bra and I just glimpse Gregory's reflection in the window. He still hasn't moved. He's watching. He wants to watch.

Sebastian is right. Gregory wants his own Willow Girl.

He wants me.

I hook two fingers into the waistband of my panties and slide them down and step out of them.

Sebastian nods in approval. He lets his gaze roam over me. It stops at my pussy and he reaches out a hand, touches the smooth skin.

"I like this."

He grips my hips and draws me closer, lifts one leg, puts my foot on his thigh and dips his head in to lick the seam of my sex. A long, slow, calculated show of ownership that makes my breath hitch.

"You're wet," he says, leaning back. "I think having my brother watch makes you wet."

I feel heat flush my face as Sebastian rises to his feet and grips my hips. He looks down at me and I see the want in his eyes.

I reach out my hands, touch them to his chest, then up to his face. When I get on tiptoe to kiss him, he takes a handful of hair and begins to wind it around his fist. He forces my head backward, so I can't kiss him, but I have to look at him.

"Do you want him?" he asks.

I search his eyes, give a quick shake of my head.

He chuckles. "Liar."

He spins me around and moves us two steps, bends me over, keeping hold of my hips.

I reach out to grip the edge of the bed as he slaps my inner thighs. I widen my legs and hear him unzip his jeans and I look up at Gregory and his eyes have gone black and he's watching us.

"Yeah. Like that," Sebastian says. "Look at him while I fuck you."

I pull away, but he catches me, and forces me back into position.

"Stop," I try.

He grips my hair and tugs my head back, making me look at Gregory. I feel the fingers of his other hand open me.

"You're dripping, Helena."

I reach back, grab his forearm, try to pry him off, but he pushes me forward, forces my face into the bed and slides his cock into me.

My body stretches for him, but that first instant, it always takes my breath away and I let out a small sound.

He lets go of my hair and his big hands close over my hips, spreading me wider. I look back at him, and he drags his gaze to mine as he pulls out, then thrusts, the force making me grunt, and I can't look away from him when he does it again, then again.

I feel a tear slide from my eye, over the bridge of my nose and drop onto the bed.

Sebastian sees it too and he stops, pulls out, turns me over onto my back. He tugs me to the edge of the bed, pushes into me, and I wrap my legs around him. He leans down over me, taking my arms wide, holding them like that, his face an inch from mine.

I raise my head, kiss him. It's a soft kiss, this first one, but the next one is deeper, and I feel him move inside me, slow and deep and he stops kissing me to turn me over again, this time on my elbows and knees on the bed and when he hooks a finger inside my ass, all I can do is feel.

I lay my cheek down and blink softly and my mouth opens as I try to suck in air and Gregory is still watching us. He's watching, and his eyes are black and his jaw is tight. His erection pushes against his pants and I arch my back and push against Sebastian, rising up a little, readying myself to be fucked, really fucked.

Wanting it.

Wanting it like this.

Sebastian curls his finger and grips me from the inside and with his other hand, he's holding me in place and fucking me hard, punishing me with each thrust, punishing me for being aroused. For wanting this.

For wanting to come while his brother watches.

And when I do, it's ecstasy and I close my eyes and feel Sebastian behind me, inside me, and he swells, and his thrusts come short and hard until he stills, and his cock is pumping inside me, emptying inside me and I want more of him, all of him, I need him to fill me up and keep me like this.

I need him to keep me.

9

SEBASTIAN

I watch my brother walk out and listen to the door click closed behind him.

Helena rolls onto her side, shifts her gaze from the door to me.

"That was cruel."

I look at her. "Letting him watch us fuck was cruel? He'll get off on it."

I slide my gaze over her before going into the bathroom to switch on the shower.

"Come here, Helena."

She obeys. She's sweet when she's obedient.

I open the shower door. It's large enough for two and I step in behind her. She closes her eyes, dips her head under the flow. I drag my gaze away to pick up the washcloth and bodywash.

She's so beautiful, sleek and wet, slender, but not soft, lean with muscle. She doesn't protest when I begin to wash her, the fucking and the water sobering me a little.

Thing is, on this day, it's hard to get drunk and harder to stay drunk.

The bruises Lucinda left have all but faded, only a few still tender, yellowing spots remaining.

"Almost ready for new marks?" she asks sarcastically when I turn her to face me.

"I won't do what she did to you. I won't hurt you like that. You know that."

"Why didn't you tell me about today?"

I duck my head under the water and she takes the washcloth from me, starts at my shoulders.

"Why didn't you tell me about this?" she asks, her fingers gentle on the stitches that need to come out soon.

"You weren't exactly chatty when you first came around, remember?"

"You mean after you kept me sedated for two weeks?"

I turn to her, set the cloth aside, take her arms. "I'm tired, Helena."

Water sprays against her face as she studies me, gives a nod.

I switch off the taps and grab a towel, wrap her in it before drying myself off and wrapping one around my hips.

She takes a second one and rubs a little of the moisture out of her hair.

"Tell me about today," she says once we get into the bedroom.

I pull back the covers on the bed and she climbs in. I follow and switch out the lights.

"What did my brother tell you?"

"That it's your birthday."

She pauses, and I wait.

Because I know that's not all.

"I know you had a twin brother. I know he died. And I know about your mother."

I snort, roll onto my back and stare up at the ceiling. A speedboat races by and someone shouts outside.

"He didn't leave anything out, did he?"

"It's my fault. I went to the mausoleum."

I turn to find her watching me, her face in shadows, her eyes glistening.

"I'm sorry you're hurting, Sebastian."

I turn back to the ceiling. "Not sorry you broke a rule?"

"Are you going to punish me?"

"No."

It's quiet for a long time but neither of us are sleeping.

"The church refused to hold mass for her. Suicide."

"Do you believe in God?"

"I used to. Now, I believe in ghosts."

"Is that why you didn't want to be inside the church that day we went to Joseph Gallo's office?"

"Yeah." I turn to her again, brush my fingers across her cheek. "I don't have many memories of her, more a feeling. She was kind and gentle and loving. She was the opposite of everything we are. In a way, she didn't belong in our family, with my father. She wasn't ever going to make it. Too soft."

I think about Helena now. She's soft too.

"She sounds wonderful."

"She was." I turn on my side, collect her to me. It's quiet again and I close my eyes.

"Sebastian?" she asks when I think we're finished. "Your brother. Where did he go?"

"Why do you care about him?"

"I'm just worried."

"Don't be. He's fine. He needs to learn his place."

"He came here to help you."

"He brought you here to fuck with me. To fuck with you."

"How's that? Because from what I saw, he rushed to get here so you wouldn't be alone."

I reach over, switch on the light. Helena blinks, and it takes a minute for her eyes to come into focus. I climb on top of her, keeping most of my weight on my forearms.

I want to see her face, her eyes. I don't want to miss a thing.

"Don't let Gregory fool you. You don't know him."

"Funny, that's what he said about you."

"Careful there, Helena."

"I just want to know where you think he went. It was cruel what you did."

"What *we* did." I push her knees apart with mine. I'm getting hard again. "You liked having him watch you. Like the other time at the pool. You liked having him touch you."

I cup the sides of her head, hug my forearms into her so she can't move as I push into her.

She makes a sound, and I know she's raw, but I don't care.

"Say it, Helena. Tell me."

She's digging her nails into my back and it hurts.

"I want you, not him," she says.

"Is that true?" I thrust hard and she grunts. "Or do you want both of us?"

She blinks, tries to turn her head away, and my next thrust is to punish her.

"Say it."

She shakes her head and I weave my fingers into her wet hair and squeeze.

"Say it."

"I'm just worried about him."

"My brother's fine. If I know Gregory, he's fucking some whore right now." I reach one arm down, grab her leg, bend her knee so I can get deeper. "You're mine, Helena. Not his. Not anyone else's."

She's slick and I feel myself thicken inside her as my thrusts come faster, matching her panting breath.

She drags her nails down my back and closes her eyes and she's breaking skin.

I grin, tap her face softly when she closes her eyes.

"Eyes open. On me. Always on me when you come, understand? You only look at me when you come."

She nods and we're both breathing harder now, and a drop of sweat falls from my forehead onto her face and I lean closer, kiss her, suck in her lower lip, our eyes still open, still locked.

"I like you like this, Helena. I like having you like this."

"I'm going to come." She whisper-cries and I watch her and feel her and when the walls of her pussy pulse around my cock, I come too, emptying inside her raw cunt, branding her with my seed, marking her on the inside and all the while, one word repeats in my head again and again and again.

Mine.

10

HELENA

The next morning, we're eating breakfast on the small terrace off our room. It's early but the city is already abuzz.

"Will you take me there? I've always wanted to see it."

"It's overrun with tourists. I'll take you when it's quieter."

"I don't mind the tourists." I bite into a croissant.

Sebastian runs his hand through his still wet hair and pours himself a second cup of coffee.

"I'll take you. Just not right now."

I want to ask why, but I have other questions today. "Okay."

I finish my juice and set the glass down.

"Why did Lucinda do what she did? Kidnap me? Leave like she did? I don't understand that. Why not just wait for the year to be up? Do what she wanted to do to me then? When it came to Ethan's turn."

"Because Ethan wasn't ever going to get you."

I'm momentarily stunned into silence.

"I don't understand. Isn't that the rule?" I ask.

"Ethan isn't my father's son."

"What?"

"What I said. That's why I went to Verona. I had final confirmation then. I didn't want to use it if I didn't have to. Ethan's more fragile than you think. I told you that already."

"What happened to him?" I remember how afraid of Sebastian he was. How he wouldn't touch me for fear of him.

"After Lucinda's discipline sessions, I used to take the boat out. A canoe I used to have. I always just went out on my own to deal with it. I didn't want her to see what she did to me. How it impacted me. I didn't want to see anyone and I didn't want anyone to see me."

He takes a minute, and I wait.

"Well, the beatings got worse after my father died. Not that he did much to stop them when he was alive, but they got worse. When I was sixteen, there was a particularly bad one. I still have scars from that one. I was ashamed. And by this time, pissed as fuck. So I invited Ethan on the boat with me."

He shakes his head, runs his hand through his

hair and is looking off like he's seeing it again. Like he's back there on that canoe.

"Ethan wasn't always shitty. I mean, he was a lot of the time, but not always. Lucinda spoiled him, doted on him. Led him to believe he was a king. But he wasn't. And after my father's death, as soon as I came of age, she knew I'd take over the family. She knew her rein was fast ending. I sometimes wonder if she didn't want to kill me outright. But that's a whole other story."

There's another, longer pause.

"Anyway, Ethan joined me on the canoe and I rowed us out. I don't like to think what my intention was."

He gets up, walks into the room, keeps his back to me.

I get up too, go to him. I think I know where this story is going.

"You were a child, Sebastian."

"No, Helena. He was a child. I was sixteen. Old enough to know better."

He sits down on the edge of the bed.

"You don't have to tell me the rest."

"I want to. I've never actually told the story and I should. I own it."

I sit beside him, watch him.

"Ethan wasn't a strong swimmer. I think he was afraid of water, but never could admit it. So, when we were out there, too far from the island for anyone to see us, I tipped the canoe."

He looks down at his lap for a minute before looking back up to me.

"I watched him struggle. I watched him sink. Watched him reach for me." He shakes his head, looks at the floor. "I watched his eyes close as he stopped struggling. By time I pulled him up, he'd gone too long without oxygen. The damage was irreversible."

"Oh, God."

He stands, shakes his head. "No, Helena, there is no god. No god would allow these things to happen. Not to Ethan. Not to you. Not to my mother. Not to all the Willow Girls who came before."

I go to him, touch his face, make him look at me. "You were sixteen years old and you were abused."

"I knew what I was doing. I knew exactly what I was doing. Ethan was innocent." He looks away again. "So now you know why he's so afraid of me. What I'm capable of. I think some part of him, some subconscious part, knows. Remembers."

He pulls away, straightens. Takes a deep breath in and a moment later, he's himself again. Like he's shoved this other part of him into some box and closed and locked the lid.

"But there's still Gregory to deal with. He is blood and he has a right to you."

SEBASTIAN IS SOMBER WHEN WE RETURN TO THE island.

The other boat is already docked, and I wonder where Gregory is. If what Sebastian said is true, that he went to find someone to fuck last night. I don't know why that bothers me.

I go to my room to change my clothes and remember my dream of my Aunt Helena. I don't know if it was a dream at all, actually, and I wonder how I forgot, but now, I stand in my closet, looking at the floorboards and remembering what she said.

I get down on my hands and knees and begin searching for the loose board, knowing it's a long shot. We're talking over seventy years ago.

It takes me three turns around the place before I find it. It's in the darkest part of the closet and I have to push all the clothes to the opposite end of the rack before I see the scratches along the short edge of one of the boards.

I try to dig my fingernail in, but only end up bending it backwards. I get up, look around. I need something thin but strong to get under it.

I go into the bathroom and find a comb. It's the closest thing I have, but it's not good enough. I don't know where my pocket knife is.

There's nothing I can use in my room. I guess he's kept all sharp objects away. But I remember when I was in Lucinda's room, she had a letter opener on her desk. I go out into the hallway, and once I've made sure no one's around, I sneak into her abandoned room.

A violent surge of anger rushes me, and it takes me a minute to get myself under control. I want to hurt her. I want to hurt he like she did me. Like she did Sebastian.

Her room is a mess, I guess no one's cleaned since she's been gone.

I hurry to the desk and when I don't see the letter opener on top, I open the drawers to search for it. I find it in the last one, slip it under my sleeve in case I run into anyone in the hallway, and breathe a sigh of relief when I'm back in my own room.

On my knees inside the closet, I wedge the letter opener between the slats and, with a little nudging, lift the board. I have a pretty good sense of smell and my stomach turns at the slight scent of decay that wafts out. I shove the thought that comes at me aside and peek into the gap and inside, I find a small notebook, rolled tight, crammed into the tight space.

I pull it out, make sure there isn't anything else then replace the floor board.

I stand, spread the clothes out over the rack and head back into my bedroom. After tucking Lucinda's letter opener into the nightstand drawer, I sit on my bed and open the notebook. I leaf through it, find that some pages have been ripped out. I wonder if she'd done that or if it was someone else. A quick glance tells me the entries are fragments, snippets of thought.

Winter

Cain gave me this notebook as a three-month anniversary gift. As if we're a couple. As if I want to be here. Besides, I know he'll make me pay for it later. He always does.

It feels like I've been here longer than three months. If I break my time up by brothers, I'm one-twelfth of the way done. I have nine more months before Cain must hand me over to his brother, Jasper.

I don't know how I'll survive those months because Cain, he has a cruelty to him. He takes pleasure from hurting me.

Jasper is different. I don't know about the youngest yet, but Jasper is different.

Cain thinks his brothers will blindly obey him. Do as they're told. He doesn't know Jasper has already had me. I let him. I let him because he was tender.

It's sick, I know. When I read that back, I want to rip that word to shreds, but he was tender, in his way.

I can't think about time in years. I'll die if I do. And I refuse to die at their hands.

I turn the page over, scroll through more entries. None are dated, only the season noted, but if her time here was like mine, she didn't know the date or the day or the year or anything. She knew morning, afternoon, night.

I flip to the next page where the handwriting is more choppy and jagged, not her pretty script.

Winter/almost Spring

He left me up on that whipping post all day after my lashing. I'm still freezing cold, still shivering. I can barely write.

And the worst was that he made Jasper do it.

I don't know if I can forgive Jasper that, but what was the alternative? If he didn't or if he was gentle, Cain threatened to shred my back.

But we were stupid. Careless. It's not Jasper's turn with me. I'm still Cain's. That's what this whipping was about, to teach us both.

I'm going to kill the bastard. I'm going to kill him.

It hurts so bad this time and the ointment Jasper snuck in here makes the open skin burn. I should have cried. If I'd cried, maybe he would have been satisfied and the whipping would have ended sooner.

But there's a way out. Jasper told me there's a way out. What I'll have to submit to, though, it terrifies me.

That passage stops abruptly leaving me curious. I scroll through several more pages to see if there's more, but I can't find details and I have to put the book down for a few minutes because too many of the entries are like this one.

Beatings.

Pain.

Hate.

I scroll through, skimming, until a dark stain on the corner of a sheet catches my eye.

Spring

We're doing it tonight. Jasper has the irons and Benjamin, the youngest Scafoni brother, will bear witness.

And probably hold me down.

I'm scared. It's going to hurt so much, but the alternative, I'm sure, is death.

Cain grows angrier and angrier by the day and his punishments leave permanent marks now.

Tonight, at midnight, I'll meet Jasper at the mausoleum. God, I hate that place. It's haunted, I swear.

And the ghosts mean me harm.

He showed me the secret door that leads to the room beneath. I am chilled thinking about it. But he'll be there waiting for me and after tonight, I'll be safe. Cain will have no choice but to give me to Jasper when I wear his mark.

I am terrified.

Six days later

I know it's six days because I've started to tally it on the back of the headboard.

I endured the marking ceremony. Benjamin signed the contract as witness. According to the Scafoni family's own rules concerning the Willow Girls, I belong to Jasper now.

Rules.

It's sick. This family is sick. These rules, I swear, have been put into place to ensure their cruelty and to guarantee our suffering.

Part of this page is missing, torn out. And the next entry is only a few lines:

This morning, I woke to news that Jasper has left the island.

Benjamin won't tell me anything.

I wonder if he's alive. If Cain didn't hurt him, or worse, for his betrayal.

And I am lost.

She doesn't describe what happened. She never says what they did, but I remember my dream of her. I remember the edge of that mark on the back of her neck and how she tried to cover it up. Is that what it was? A mark of ownership?

I endured the marking ceremony.

The thought of cattle being branded crosses my mind.

It's what Willow Girls are. Property. Living, breathing property.

Cattle.

I kneel up on the bed, touch behind the heavy wooden headboard. I can feel ridges, the lines she carved into the wood to mark the days.

Getting off the bed, I shove it forward a little. It must weigh a ton, but I can see the scratches Aunt Helena left. It makes me feel like she's here again. Here with me. Like I'm not alone.

Shoving the bed back in place, I resume my seat and pick up the notebook to read the passage again.

There's a secret room under the mausoleum? I have to go there, search for it. I have to find out what they did to free her from Cain.

I read a few more entries, then get to this one:

Summer

They did it.

I couldn't write the plan here because I think Cain has been reading my journal. How could I have thought, for one single moment, that he wouldn't? That was my own stupidity. It's exactly the reason he gave it to me.

But they did it and it doesn't matter! He's dead. Cain is dead.

I heard the brothers from my room. Heard them enter, heard the struggle, heard Cain's muffled cries. It didn't even take long.

I went into his room after they'd gone. He looked like he was just sleeping but he had no breath and his color was already graying and I stood over him and smiled a real smile for the first time since I was brought to this island.

And then I did something terrible.

I took the dagger he keeps in the nightstand. I know about it because he held it to my throat enough times. He liked that when he had me. Liked scaring the life out of me. It made the sick bastard come.

Well, tonight, I took his knife and I put his hand on the nightstand and I cut off his finger and I didn't even care that I had blood on me. They'll accuse me of killing him anyway. I didn't care.

I took it back to my room and peeled the skin off like I'd peel a potato and flushed it down the toilet and I carried those bloody, wet bones to my secret place and hid them.

And I don't even care what they do to me. I don't care because now, I have a piece of them.

This is my victory, even if I am not free, because my time here isn't over. Not by a long shot.

It's the last passage in the book, even though about a third of it is still empty pages.

I put the notebook down and rub my face. I feel a little sick. I wonder if I could do that. If I could cut off Sebastian's finger. If I could hurt him.

I don't think I could.

I don't want to.

Were the Scafoni men of generations past crueler than those of today? Brother pitted against brother, that's what this does. The fact that the right of one brother can be challenged by another, that alone sets the stage for a family to turn on itself.

If I think about Lucinda and what she did to Sebastian, what Sebastian did to Ethan, it's brutal. Then there's the competition between Gregory and Sebastian.

This family is sick.

They're rotten and rotting from the inside.

And I don't understand why I am not repelled by them. Repulsed by them.

Why I'm drawn to them.

Instead of hiding the book back in the floorboards, I tuck it between the mattress and the box spring and lay down. I'm tired. Between last night's events and this, I'm exhausted.

I lie on my side for a while just watching the breeze softly blow the curtains. And when I close my eyes, I dream. I dream of my Aunt Helena, except I'm not sure if it's her or me. I'm seeing through her eyes, opening the door between my room and Sebastian's.

Gregory doesn't see me when I walk in to watch him hold a pillow over Sebastian's face.

He doesn't hear me when I step closer. There's no sound, in fact, not even when he pulls the pillow away and I see it's not Sebastian at all, but someone else, another man who resembles them.

Cain?

I'm confused as I watch Gregory leave. And I have to force my unwilling legs to carry me closer, closer.

I feel my mouth stretch into a wide grin but I'm sick. I feel sick.

The skin of my hand, when it reaches for the nightstand drawer is like parchment, spotted and old, the yellowing nails bitten down and jagged.

I open the drawer, and inside is my pocket knife. I take it out but it's like I'm resisting myself, like my arm is struggling against itself, but the pull is too great and I'm too weak and when the other hand, this one mine, takes up the dead man's hand and brings it to the nightstand, tears drop on that dead hand, even as the fingers are splayed out.

The switchblade is opened, and I turn away from it, turn to the man on the bed and when I see him, when I see Sebastian, I scream.

I scream and scream and scream until I'm startled awake, jolted upright in my own bed, the room dark, pitch black. The cool breeze of earlier now chilling, freezing.

I switch on the lamp and rub my face.

It was a dream. Just a dream.

11

SEBASTIAN

"Mind telling me what the fuck last night was about?"

I push another log into the fireplace before turning to answer my brother. Fall is fast approaching, and I like these cooler temperatures.

I straighten, turn to him. I take my time looking at him. I've known Gregory since he was a baby. Always liked him better than Ethan but that's probably because Lucinda liked him about a hair more than she did me.

But I don't *know* my brother.

"I could ask you the same thing," I say, turning, pouring myself a whiskey.

"Haven't you had enough?" Greg asks when I hold up the bottle, asking if he wants one.

"Never enough, brother. Am I pouring for you or

not?"

"Yeah."

I hand him his glass and we stand drinking, eyes locked, tension thick enough to slice.

"Last night was me making sure you know she's mine."

"You going to try to take me out of the picture too? Like you did Ethan?"

I hear the accusation underneath the last part of that remark and I feel my eyes narrow.

I've never told anyone the specifics of what happened with Ethan. No one knows but Helena. No one saw. Lucinda accused me, but there was no evidence.

But Gregory? He's never asked.

And I know for as silent as he is, he sees everything. Always has.

I turn to the fire, sip my drink. "You know what would have happened if I handed her over to him."

"I'm not saying you did the wrong thing, but I'm not Ethan. Or Lucinda. And you're wrong." He sits down at his place at the table. "I don't want her," he finishes. "Not like you think."

"I see how you look at her," I say, coming toward the table.

He shifts his gaze to me as I take my seat. "Yeah, well, when you fuck her in front of me, how do you want me to look at her? I'm human, Sebastian. I'm a man. Besides, we made an agreement. And I'm not walking away next time."

"I was out of my head last night," I say by way of apology for something, I'm not sure what.

"No kidding. But I'm not the enemy."

I drink a long swallow of whiskey before meeting his gaze.

"Thank you for taking care of her."

He nods. He's still pissed, though. I can see it on his face. But we both hear the clicking of shoes from inside the house and turn to find Helena coming outside. She's wearing skinny jeans and a gray sweater over top and has the sleeves pulled down into her palms.

"It's cold," she says, and walks to stand with her back to the fire.

I watch her, and she's being careful to keep her eyes on me.

Gregory, on the other hand, is looking straight at her, drinking his drink. I wonder if he's remembering last night.

Her on her hands and knees getting fucked.

Her coming.

"We can eat inside if you're cold," I offer.

She shakes her head. "No, it's fine. I like it out here. I'm just surprised how quickly it cools off all of a sudden." She walks over to take her seat and clears her throat before quickly meeting Greg's eyes and even more quickly blinking away.

Gregory leans back in his seat, one corner of his mouth curving upward. His words replay in my head.

"I'm not walking away next time."

I get up to pour wine for everyone and dinner is served. It's probably one of the most awkwardly silent meals we've had since Helena's been on the island.

By the time we're finished, we've also emptied two bottles of red, much of it into Helena's glass. I want her relaxed tonight for what needs to happen.

When the girl comes to clear, I tell her we won't be having dessert. I speak in Italian and although Helena doesn't understand, Gregory does, and he gives me a look.

Helena shudders, hugging her arms to herself.

"Let's go inside," I say, standing, pulling out her seat.

Once in the living room, I pour whiskey for each of us.

Helena looks between the two of us when I offer her a glass.

"I may go to bed," she says.

"It's early. Stay."

She opens her mouth to retort, but I push the glass toward her.

"You'll stay."

She studies my eyes, cautiously takes the glass and drinks a sip.

Gregory is sitting on one end of the sofa, leaning back, relaxed.

I take the other end.

Helena stands awkwardly.

"Here." I point to the space between us.

"What are you doing?" she asks.

"Offering you a seat."

She's quiet.

"Sit down," I say.

She sits.

"Drink your drink."

"I don't like it."

"Drink it anyway."

She does. She drinks it all down and holds out her empty glass. "Happy?"

I take it, set it aside, shrug a shoulder.

"Now can I go?" she asks.

"No."

We lock eyes and I know she knows what's coming. What I want to happen. And she's scared.

I reach out, cup the back of her head with one hand and pull her in to kiss me.

She pushes against my chest and keeps her lips tightly sealed.

I draw back, look at her, my hand still on the back of her head, holding her by her hair. I drink my whiskey and turn her, push her toward my brother.

"You don't kiss her mouth."

Gregory nods.

I wish I could see her face. I see his. And he's as unreadable as ever.

He takes a long swallow of his whiskey before setting his glass down and reaching to place his hand where mine was. He pulls her to him and she shoves back, harder than she did with me. He fists her hair and with his other hand, undoes the top button of her jeans.

She catches his arm, but he tugs her head backward, closes his mouth over her throat and she lets out a desperate sound.

Gregory pulls back, eyes dark, searching her face before handing her back to me.

"What are you doing?" she asks, rising to her feet.

I rise too, keeping hold of her hair with one hand, unzipping her jeans with the other and sliding my hand inside to cup her pussy.

I lean in close, rub once. "I just want to see if you're wet," I whisper loud enough for my brother to hear.

Gregory gets up, goes to the liquor cart and pours himself more whiskey before resuming his seat, knees spread wide, leaning back, his arm draped over the side of the couch as he sips, never taking his eyes off her.

"Is she?" he asks.

I rub again, watch her eyes widen, see the color flush her cheeks. I smile.

"Oh yeah. You should feel for yourself."

I pull my hand out and push her toward my brother.

"Sebastian," she starts.

"Quiet, Willow Girl."

She turns her face to me. "What are you doing?"

"Quiet or I'll gag you and I'd really like to be able to use your mouth."

Gregory takes hold of her by the waist of her jeans, stealing her attention.

She lets out a little cry when he tugs them and her panties down to mid-thigh. His eyes drop to her naked pussy for a moment before he gets to his feet and steps toward her, closing his big hand over her sex.

Her breathing is short and when he wraps his other hand around the back of her neck, I release her and pick up my own glass to finish my drink before refreshing it.

I watch them. Watch him kiss her temple, her cheek, the line of her jaw, everything but her mouth. I watch him rub her clit. Watch her face change, her mouth opening, watch her push into his hand.

I set my glass aside and pull off my sweater.

Greg turns her to me and leans down to pull her jeans and panties off before rising to draw her sweater over her head, unhook her bra and strip her bare.

I pull her to me, kiss her, cup her pussy while

Gregory strips off his shirt and kisses the back of her neck, the curve of her shoulder, her back.

I collect her hair and lift it up, tilt her head so her ear is to my mouth. "When you come, you only come with me, understand? And you look only at me."

She nods, her eyes wide.

"Undo my jeans," I tell her.

She does, her fingers fumbling a little.

"Now take me out."

She reaches in, cups my cock and draws it out, her hungry eyes locked on mine.

"Good girl. Do the same for my brother."

She turns, is a little more hesitant with him.

He leans in, pushes her hair from her ear, cups the back of her neck. "I don't bite," he whispers, taking the lobe of her ear between his teeth, grinning as he counters what he just said.

She gasps, her hands on his chest, trembling as they travel down over his belly to undo his jeans.

I wrap my hand around to rub her pussy, taking her clit between thumb and forefinger and kissing her shoulder.

"That's it. You're doing good," I say.

Gregory has a one-sided grin on his face and waits patiently as she takes his jeans down, looks down at his ready cock. Cups it and licks her lips.

I put one hand on her shoulder and push her to her knees and she opens her mouth and takes him in and Gregory puts one hand on the top of her head like he's blessing her.

He closes his eyes and exhales a breath.

I move to sit on the couch, picking up my whiskey, drinking, watching her suck his cock, watching as he cups the back of her head and holds her as he pushes in deeper.

She resists, pushing against his thighs.

Gregory's hand fists in her hair, holds her in place.

"Easy, brother. Mine's the first dick she sucked."

"So, she's *almost* a virgin," Gregory says, easing out of her mouth, sitting on the sofa and picking up his drink.

Helena remains kneeling between us.

"You don't make her come unless I say," I tell Gregory. "And you don't kiss her mouth. Ever."

"Understood." He sets his drink down. "Stand up," he tells her.

Helena glances at me and I give her a nod. She stands.

"Now come here."

Obediently, she goes to him.

He takes hold of her hips and pulls her closer, using his thumbs to open the lips of her wet pussy. He leans his head in and licks and she gasps and grips his shoulders to remain standing.

With one tug, he has her straddling him, her knees on either side of his thighs. He takes one nipple into his mouth and she's still holding onto his shoulders, watching the top of his head and a moment later, he draws back to look at me.

"Fuck her cunt. I want her ass."

I stand up, move behind her and wrap her hair around my fist, turn her to look at me, kiss her as my brother draws her down, and the moment he sheathes himself on her, I steal her exhale, swallow it.

"She's tight, brother," Greg says, his voice husky.

"She is. Tight and wet." I knead her nipple, turning it between my fingers. When her breath hitches, I squeeze. "If you come on his dick, I'll punish you, understand?"

She nods and Greg smiles.

I disappear into the kitchen, return a moment later with the bottle of olive oil and push my jeans and briefs off.

Gregory grips her hips and drops to his knees on the floor.

I kneel behind her, listening to her as I rub olive oil all over my dick and I know it takes all she has not to come right now. I can hear it in the way she breathes, in the wet sounds of her cunt.

"Soon, Helena," I say.

She turns her head back and kisses me. "I can't. Please."

I give a shake of my head. "You'd better." With

that, I close my mouth over hers and smear olive oil over her tight little asshole.

She mewls. Begs again.

"Fuck, she's going to come," Greg says. "I feel it."

I slap Helena's ass with one hand while pushing one slick finger into her ass.

"You ready to take us both?"

She nods because she's on the edge.

She leans forward a little, offering me her ass as she grips Greg's shoulders.

I press a second finger to smear the oil inside her. I look at my brother, give a nod and he pulls out and when he does, I push in and she cries out in pain or pleasure or both.

Greg cups her face, watches her for a moment before turning it, kissing her neck just beneath her ear as I push deeper, and she cries out again, her tight ass squeezing my cock.

"Let me in, Helena. Relax."

I reach around, rub her soaking clit and a moment later, she has her first orgasm and I push in as she does, and she throws her head back onto my shoulder and I see her nails digging into my brother's shoulders and her eyes are closed and she's coming so hard, I won't be able to hold on for long.

"Fuck."

I'm all the way in and I hold there for a minute, enjoying the tight squeeze of her asshole before pulling out a little as Greg pushes into her pussy.

Helena's falling apart begging for more, begging for us to stop, clinging to Gregory, reaching for me and we fuck her hard and fast and she's never empty, not until we both blow inside her, her cunt and ass stretched tight, taking both of us, shuddering with her own orgasm until she slumps forward over Gregory's shoulder, her arms dropping to her sides, limp, and useless.

12

HELENA

Gregory pulls out first and when he does, I feel the rush of cum, his and mine, slide out of me.

I blink away, his gaze too intense, too much.

He's beautiful when he comes. His eyes go soft. It's the only time they do that.

I watched him, just for a little. I know Sebastian said eyes on him, but I had to.

Sebastian slides out of me and I have to hold on to Gregory when he does. I'm so sensitive right now. Everything is throbbing, and I know if they touch me again, I'll break apart.

I turn in Sebastian's arms, meet his eyes as he stands, lifts me with him. I can't read him. I can't ever read him. I turn my face into his chest, soft skin over hard muscle. I inhale the scent of him, feel his strength as he, without a word, walks to the stairs and begins to climb them.

When I open my eyes, it's to look back to see Gregory there, watching us.

His eyes find mine and hold them, just for a moment, before he breaks our gaze and walks outside and all I can think is that he's alone. Even after this, he's still alone.

Sebastian carries me to his room, lays me on his bed.

I start to rise. "I need to shower."

He shakes his head, slips in beside me. "I like the smell of sex on you. I like knowing my cum is still inside you."

I lean up, kiss him, but he pulls back.

"I know," he says.

"Know what?"

"I know you looked back. You looked back at him."

He sees everything.

"And you looked at him when you came."

"I wanted to watch him come. He's beautiful. Like you."

And lonely, I think.

I think that more and more.

Sebastian doesn't say anything, and I sit up, lean my back against the headboard, and the soreness reminds me how he had me. How they both had me.

"What are we doing?" I ask him.

He studies my eyes, and I, his.

"Fucking," he says, his tone harder. He gets up, goes into the bathroom. I hear water run and he returns a moment later drying himself. He remains standing.

"It's not just fucking."

"What is it, then?"

"I don't know. He's alone, Sebastian."

"Do you want to go to him?"

"No."

"Good."

"But he's alone."

"You looked at him when you came."

I don't reply but what I see in his eyes, it reflects my own confusion. Like he's somehow torn.

"Why did you look at him?"

"I wanted to see."

His forehead creases, he's trying to understand.

"Punish me," I say.

He's still for a long time.

"Punish me for it."

He seems to think about this for a long time until he finally gives me a nod and sits on the edge of the bed.

"Come here, Helena."

I slide off the bed and go to him, stand between his knees. He takes my hands, looks at me for the longest time and I feel tears build behind my eyes. I don't know why, though.

What we did, he wanted it. I wanted it. But this, him looking at me like this, Sebastian the most cruel and the most tender. I don't understand my feelings for him. I don't understand this confusion of emotions, this warring inside me.

"Punish me," I say again, tears warming my face.

He draws me over his lap so my torso is resting on the bed and my legs are hanging off his thighs. He scissors his legs to trap mine between his and takes both of my wrists into one of his hands at the small of my back. He then rubs one cheek, then the other and when he slaps the flat of his hand over one, I gasp and think I need this.

It's a cleansing. A sort of contrition.

And maybe he needs it too.

He brings his hand down again and again, two on one cheek, then two on the other, and it stings more than I think it should and although I don't want to struggle, although I want to take it, he still has to squeeze his legs together to keep mine trapped and the hand that's gripping my wrists is firm, just shy of bruising.

It's loud, the spanking. Louder than my cries which are more whimpers.

I'm biting my lip to take it, and I don't know if when I cry it's because it hurts or because I just need to, need to let out the strange emotions inside me.

And I know when he punishes me, it's not only

for my wanting his brother, or for watching him come, or for letting him watch me.

It's because he wanted this too. Because he gave me to him.

When I'm too tired to struggle anymore and my arms and legs go limp, he stops.

"Enough?"

I nod.

I'm exhausted and I just want him to hold me and when he raises me up to cradle me against him, I turn my face into his chest and I cry. I cry deep, quiet sobs. I don't understand the reason for them. I don't understand all these mixed-up emotions.

When it's finally over, I reach up, sit up, and he's still watching me. With his hands on either side of my face, he uses his thumbs to wipe away my tears before kissing me. And when he cups the back of my head, his touch is gentle.

"You're mine. Even when he fucks you, you're mine."

I nod. "I know that. I know."

He's hard, I feel him between my legs and when he lifts my hips and lowers me onto him, all I can do is cling to him, our eyes locked, close, so close.

It's not urgent, this fucking. It's him reclaiming me, fucking me where his brother just fucked me. Where his brother just came inside me. Fucking me deep and slow and when he comes, I touch his face and just look at him. I can't look away and I don't come. I just watch him and what I'm feeling, it's twisted. It makes no sense.

When he's still, and he's holding me, I run my fingers through his hair.

"You're beautiful," I say.

He gives a small smile and when we sleep that night, we're both clinging to one another, naked, the room smelling of sex, of us, his gentle heartbeat lulling me to sleep, his soft breath on the top of my head, arms around me, cocooning me.

———

THE NEXT MORNING, IT'S CLOSE TO ELEVEN WHEN I wake up. After a shower, I go downstairs, trying to push the memory of last night out of my head.

I don't know what I feel. A little embarrassed at it all. A little hungover from the wine and the whiskey. A lot raw from the fucking.

The spanking, it wasn't a punishment at all. It was a purging.

I feel different this morning, but it's not lighter. I remember what Gregory said to me when they brought me back to the island. That it's just us now. That things are changing.

I can't think about a time that Sebastian will give me to Gregory. A time that I'll belong to Gregory. I don't think I'll be able to stand it, Sebastian here with us, but me, not with him. Not in his bed. Not in his arms.

It makes no sense, what I feel, because being with them last night, I liked it. We were close. So close. And then, Sebastian and me...

I'm so confused and the word that keeps coming up, that one word to describe what I'm feeling, it can't be that.

I give my head a shake.

Right now, I just have to focus on how I'm going to get through the morning. How I'm going to look Gregory in the eye.

But the moment I get outside, I find a note addressed to me sitting on top of the plate in my place. I pick it up, unfold it.

Helena,

Gregory and I are off the island for an appointment. You're on your own for the day. We have a party tonight. I need you ready by eight o'clock for a late dinner. Dress will be sent up later today. Wear your hair up.

S

Okay. I guess I'm relieved, at least for the time being.

I eat a leisurely breakfast and spend the afternoon swimming and reading. I even fall asleep poolside and by the time seven o'clock rolls around, I'm a little bored, so I go upstairs to get ready.

The dress is a beautiful floor length, strapless, white dress with a flowing skirt and long slit that reaches a little higher than mid-thigh. On the bodice and part of the skirt are butterflies in various shades of turquoise and sea-blue some with wings wide open, some resting, all beautiful.

The high-heeled sandals that come with the dress are about as comfortable as I'd expect but the whole look is beautiful, right down to the diamond studs and bracelet that go with them.

For the first time in what feels like forever, I put on makeup, lining my eyes heavily in black, and twisting my hair into an elegant chignon. I look different than usual. Older and more sophisticated.

I go downstairs in the hopes of having a drink to calm my nerves because I keep thinking about last night.

The living room is dark, and I don't switch on any lights, but the moment I reach for the bottle of vodka, someone clears their throat behind me.

My back stiffens, and I startle.

Goosebumps cover my flesh and my nipples seem to harden in the suddenly cool room.

Before I can move, Gregory is behind me. He takes the bottle from me and pours me a glass.

"Ice?"

I shake my head. I smell his aftershave and he's

so close, I can feel his breath on the back of my naked neck.

He holds the glass out to me.

"Thank you," I say, taking it, his fingers warm against mine.

He surprises me when he walks away, back to his seat. I turn and remain where I am. I need the distance.

He lets his gaze run over me. "You look good."

"Thank you."

"Did you have a nice day?" he asks, swirling the amber liquid around his glass.

I nod. Swallow a big gulp. Almost choke on it.

He must notice because he chuckles. "Do I make you nervous, Helena?"

He didn't call me Willow Girl. That's good, right?

"No," I say.

"You sure?"

I nod. "Where's Sebastian?" I ask.

"Come here," he says instead of answering me and pats the seat beside him.

"I'm fine."

"Come here." His tone makes a command out of the words and I go. I sit beside him. "Don't worry, I can't touch you when Sebastian isn't in the room."

"Is that some sort of agreement you two made?"

"Yeah."

"I'm glad you consulted me."

"Why would we need to consult our Willow Girl?"

Ah. There it is.

"*My* Willow Girl," Sebastian's voice booms.

I startle, gasp.

Sebastian is standing at the entrance of the room wearing a tux.

"*Your* Willow Girl," Gregory says, getting to his feet. He doesn't seem ruffled, though.

"Don't forget that, brother."

"You'd never let me, brother."

I stand up too. "What's the party?"

"A little thing Gallo's throwing."

"Joseph Gallo? Why are we going? You don't even like him."

"I don't trust him. Like has nothing to do with it."

"Then why are we going?"

"Because he invited us."

"Why do I have to go?"

"Because you look pretty on my arm. Let's go."

He holds out his hand.

I go to him, take it. At the door, he puts a wrap around my shoulders that matches the dress.

"You look beautiful."

"Thank you."

We go out to the boat and tonight, I ride inside while the brothers ride outside, Gregory smoking a cigarette. It brings back memories of the night Lucinda had me kidnapped and I look away.

But when we dock at the same spot where Sebastian and I came when I had to sign that stupid ledger, I hesitate.

"Where's the party?"

"At our property," Sebastian says, obviously waiting to tell me until the last minute.

"I don't want to go there." I back away from him.

Gregory makes a noise and steps off the boat onto the dock.

"We're both here with you, Helena. Nothing's going to happen."

"Please. I don't think I can."

Sebastian takes my hand, holds it tight in his. "I promise I'm not going to let anything happen to you."

"I don't have a choice, do I?"

He doesn't answer. He doesn't have to.

With Gregory on one side of me, and Sebastian on the other, we head to the building and I wonder how Lucinda and Ethan got me to it without anyone seeing. It's a little bit of a walk from the dock.

As we get closer, I grow more nauseous, and when we're climbing the stairs, Sebastian has to all but drag me up.

The doors open to a beautifully lit space and soft opera music playing in the background.

The gathering is small, maybe forty people, and a long dining table is set formally. Gold and white are apparently the theme and I recognize the receptionist who greeted us last time.

We've just taken three glasses of champagne from a passing waiter when Joseph Gallo makes his way toward us.

I stiffen and slide my hand into Sebastian's.

He squeezes it.

"Sebastian. Gregory," he says, shaking their hands, smiling wide. "And Helena. Pleasure to see you again."

I don't offer my hand.

"Helena, why don't we go find some food," Gregory says, taking my arm.

I look to Sebastian, but he's got his eyes locked on Gallo.

"Come on," Gregory says.

I let him lead me away. I turn to him and he seems relaxed, picking up a canape and chewing on it, replacing his already empty champagne glass with something stronger.

"What's going on?" I ask.

"Gallo has the only key to that room Lucinda put you in."

"He knew?"

"Possibly more than that. Watch closely."

I do. I can see from here the older man lose his cool, flustered maybe for the first time in his life. Sebastian stands tall and proud and powerful, a force to be reckoned with.

"Do you think he knows where Lucinda and Ethan are?"

"Not sure," Gregory says, eating another bite of something.

"How can you eat right now?" I ask, turning to him.

He shrugs a shoulder. "I'm hungry."

A woman approaches us, older, but quite beautiful and elegant, and I glance up at Gregory, who seems to roll his eyes.

"Jacqueline, you look lovely, as always," he says, taking her offered hand and kissing it.

The woman smiles, cocks her head and gives me a sideways glance. But she isn't interested in me.

"I haven't seen you in a long time, Gregory. I've missed you."

"I've had a guest, this is Helena Willow. From the states."

"Oh. Pleasure." I can see from her face it's anything but. She turns back to Gregory and follows his eyes to Sebastian and Gallo. She grins. "Your brother seems to be in rare form. I'll go say hello to him since you seem occupied with your guest."

Gregory grabs her arm. "I wouldn't do that just yet."

She looks at him, confused for a moment. He gives her a smile.

"I'll see you later tonight, Jacqueline."

With that, he dismisses her, and I turn to him.

"Do you fuck her or something? Isn't she a little old for you?"

"Some might say you're a little young for me."

"I'm only a few years younger than you."

"She's only a few years older."

"Besides, I'm not *for* you."

He leans in close, cups my ass. "I don't remember you shoving me away when you were coming on my dick last night."

I hate that his comment flusters me, leaves me feeling embarrassed and at a loss.

"Why did he spank you?" he asks, his expression changing, becoming serious.

I feel myself flush red. Again.

"Spankings are loud. I have ears," he says.

"None of your business."

"Tell me anyway."

I look at his dark eyes, so similar to Sebastian's yet so different. "I asked him to."

"Why?"

"Because I looked at you when I came."

He's quiet, considering. I guess he doesn't expect me to be as direct as he can be. "Why did you?"

I shake my head, shrug my shoulder and look at the middle of his chest for a second. "I don't know. It was just where I was looking."

"Bullshit."

I shift my gaze to his eyes. "What do you want me to say?"

"The truth."

"And what do you think that is?"

"You like me watching you. You like watching me. And you like being fucked by both of us."

I don't know how to answer that. It's the truth, after all. Gregory speaks the truth.

"Difference is, you sleep in his bed," he says.

"I'm his."

"Because you have to be or because you want to be?"

"Both."

"And what about me? What about how you look at me?"

His gaze shifts to somewhere beyond me, and I turn to find Sebastian approach with Gallo in tow. He looks at the both of us before signaling to Gregory that we should follow, and I'm saved from having to answer.

Sebastian and Gallo go ahead of us up the stairs and Gregory follows with his hand at my low back.

When we reach Gallo's office, he unlocks the door and we all enter. He moves behind his desk, opens a drawer. From inside it, he pulls out a CD or DVD. Sebastian takes it, pockets it.

"Are there copies?"

"No."

"Did you watch it?"

Gallo glances at me, shakes his head no.

Sebastian steps close to the older man, takes him by the collar and lifts him.

Considering everything I've been through with Sebastian, this is the most violent I've seen him and it's startling.

"I'll throw you out the fucking window if I find out you had anything to do with this."

"I didn't. I told you. I was the one who told you where she was, remember?"

He was?

"That doesn't prove innocence."

"How many times do you want me say it? I questioned the girl and she said Lucinda had asked her for a copy of the key for storage purposes. She didn't know any better and your mother—"

"Stepmother."

"Your stepmother can be persistent. I only bothered to look at the video at all when I noticed my key was missing."

"You keep your keys on you."

"Not that one. There's no need. No one ever goes down there."

"Fine."

Sebastian releases the older man, and Gallo stumbles backward, rights himself and adjusts his collar.

"Get out," Sebastian says.

We watch as Gallo leaves, closing the door behind him.

"I really wanted to see you throw him out the window," Gregory says. He's sitting on one of the chairs, casual, his ankle crossed over his other knee.

Sebastian leans on the front of the desk, folds his arms and looks from Gregory to me.

"What were you two talking about downstairs?"

"Nothing," I say too quickly.

He narrows his eyes. He knows I'm lying.

"I was asking her why you spanked her last night."

"What?" Sebastian starts, not sounding surprised. "Did you jerk off to the thought of it, brother?" he asks, taking a step toward Gregory.

"No need," Greg says, standing and taking a step toward his brother so they're nose to nose. "I'd had my fill."

"I should throw *you* out the fucking window." Sebastian takes hold of Gregory's shirt.

"I'd like to see you try." Gregory's response matches Sebastian's and the two turn a circle.

"What are you doing?" I ask, trying to step between them. "Having some sort of pissing contest?"

Neither looks at me and I put one hand on each of their fists.

"You need to mark your territory or something?" I continue, trying to yank them off each other.

"We already established territory," Sebastian says, his eyes on his brother.

"I thought we had too," Gregory says. "But you keep going back on our agreement."

"What agreement?" I ask.

Nothing.

"What agreement?" I ask again.

For a minute, I think they're going to fight, and I think that yes, one of them will throw the other out the window.

But then Gregory says something in Italian and Sebastian exhales.

He gives me a glance because whatever Gregory just said diffused things.

They release each other and I find myself exhaling.

"What agreement?" I ask once more a moment later.

"You, Helena," Greg answers, eyes on his brother. "You're the agreement."

13

SEBASTIAN

I look at Helena, then at my brother and in that minute, I hate him. I hate him for what he proposed. Because there is a way out. A way for Helena to be mine. For this to be over without breaking tradition. Without consequences for the next generation of Scafoni sons.

But I'm not entertaining that. No fucking way. Even if she agreed, I wouldn't allow it.

My dick is hard at the thought, though. That's the sickest part of this. And my brother knows it.

"What did he say?" She has her hands on the lapels of my jacket.

When I don't answer but keep my gaze on my brother she turns to him.

"What did you say?" she asks him.

Gregory's gaze is burning daggers into me.

Does he want it? Does he want that for her?

"We're leaving," I say to her, taking her by the arm. She stumbles when I lead the way to the door.

She looks back at Gregory once we're out in the hallway and it pisses me off.

I stop.

"You want to go back?" I ask, giving her a shake.

"No. Christ. I can't even look at him without you thinking I want him?"

"I know him, Helena."

"You're brothers, Sebastian. That means something because from what I can see, you need each other."

"You have no fucking idea what you're saying."

We make it down the stairs without her toppling and when we're outside, she stops.

"At least let me take these off."

She reaches down to remove the sandals. Like glass slippers. Like she's Cinderella.

When we're back on the boat, she stops me. "You can't leave him there."

"He'll get back. He always does. Can't manage to lose the son of a bitch."

"Sebastian, you don't mean that."

"How do you know what I mean?" I snap. The look on her face is stunned and I run a hand through my hair, take a deep breath in. "Fuck." I shake my head. "Go inside and sit down. Give me some space. I need to cool down."

Remarkably, she does as she's told and goes

inside. It's probably the cold as much as anything else, though. She must have dropped her wrap when we were in Gallo's office.

Before Helena, Gregory and I didn't fight. We weren't best friends or anything, but we didn't fight. Not like this. This Willow Girl thing, it's driving a wedge between us and it's like an echo of Lucinda's words on the night of the reaping.

It's history repeating itself.

It happens with every generation.

When we finally get back, Helena goes upstairs, and I head out to the patio. After taking off my jacket and bowtie, I stack wood in the fire and light it before sitting down with my whiskey. I look at my brother's empty chair.

Helena returns a few minutes later wearing jeans and a long-sleeved sweater. She's barefoot and when she sits, she tucks her knees under herself.

"Are you okay?" she asks.

"You're right. We're brothers. And I'm letting this thing come between us."

"This thing. Me."

I nod. Drink. Offer her my glass.

She shakes her head.

"I think he's just lonely, Sebastian. I think he's alone."

"You two are chummy."

"It's not like that. I thought he was a jerk in the beginning. I mean, he still is, a lot of the time. But when I talk to him, I also think he's lonely. I don't know, maybe I'm wrong."

She's not wrong. I know that.

The sound of swiftly approaching footsteps alerts us both to his arrival.

I glance up to find Gregory with his tie undone, his forehead creased, holding Helena's wrap. It looks strange in his hand, the feminine, pretty cashmere wrap.

I pick up the whiskey and pour him a glass.

Helena gets up, takes the wrap from Gregory.

"I'll go upstairs and let you two talk."

"Stay," I say.

My brother takes his glass, sits.

Helena watches us, sits on the hearth with her back close to the fire. Her little toenails are painted a muted pink. I wonder when she did that.

It takes a few minutes before we start talking. We're both looking into the fire and not at each other and not at Helena. And neither of us mentions what just happened. What's been happening for a while now.

"You believe Gallo?" Gregory asks.

"I don't know. It makes sense that Lucinda would bully the girl into giving her a copy of the key. I just wonder what would have happened if he hadn't realized his key was missing in the first place. What would have happened if the girl had put it back and he never noticed."

I see Helena is watching me from my periphery. She knows what I'm talking about.

"I don't think she meant to kill her," Gregory says. He turns to Helena. "Sorry."

"Who knows with her. She's just crazy enough and she had nothing more to lose. Not after trying to shoot me."

"Get you out of the way before you share your information and out Ethan. Take away any claim he has to the Scafoni inheritance."

"I wasn't ever going to out him. That was the point. That was why I went to her in the first place."

"Yeah, well," Gregory starts, emptying his glass. "Lucinda's got history with the Willow Girls."

Helena shudders.

I turn to Greg, put my hand on his shoulder. This next part I say in Italian. I don't want Helena to understand. "I stand by what we agreed. I don't ever want you to bring up the alternative."

Helena perks up, her forehead creases in annoyance.

Gregory nods and we drink a second glass.

I look at Helena.

"I want to watch," I say.

Her skin flushes and her gaze drifts to Gregory who is gazing into the fire.

"Same rules. No kissing on the mouth," I tell Greg, then turn to her. "And if you come, I'll punish you." I know it's not fair, but I don't care.

Her throat works as she swallows, and Gregory takes one more sip before getting to his feet. Helena looks up at him and I like this difference in size. She's so small next to us. So fragile.

He holds out his hand.

She studies it for a long minute before placing her smaller one inside his and rising to stand on her bare feet.

Greg walks her to the long table.

I lean back in my chair, cross one ankle over my other knee.

He noisily shoves a chair out of the way and tugs Helena to stand before it. He doesn't bother to strip her, just pushes her sweater way up, slides the cups of the bra under her tits and drags his nails across them before turning her so she's facing me and pushing her to bend over the table.

He then unceremoniously shoves her jeans and panties down and off, and nudges at her knee with one of his so she spreads her legs.

She steps out of both jeans and panties and complies, and he looks down at her and I know what he sees. Her perfect ass, round and full, her long slender legs.

Before touching her, he takes off his jacket and tosses it over the arm of the chair he just shoved aside, then tugs his tie off and drops it on top. He unbuttons the top buttons of his shirt and pulls it out of his slacks before undoing his belt, letting it hang open as he nudges her knees wider and steps between them, leans over her for a moment, taking her arms and stretching them out to either side.

She turns her cheek and he first kisses it then her neck.

"Eyes on my brother," he whispers loud enough that I hear it.

She does as he says, and I hold her midnight blue gaze, my dick hard when she licks her lips, anticipating.

It's going to be very hard for her to not come.

Gregory straightens, puts his hands on her ass, draws her open. He looks at her, and I imagine him seeing her pretty little asshole, her cunt which, from the look on her face, is already wet. He runs his fingers over her clit up through her pussy and if I know my brother, he's smearing her juices onto her asshole.

Helena shifts from foot to foot and arches her back. She's gripping the sides of the table.

"Remember, Helena. If you come, you'll be punished."

She makes a sound, nods, looks away for a minute.

"We'll know," I add, just in case she thinks we won't.

Gregory snorts, unzips his pants, fists his cock.

I watch her face as he smears it in her juices, rubbing himself over her clit, her cunt, her ass, and I know the instant he slides into her pussy and it takes all I have not to grip my own cock, pump it as I watch my brother fuck my Willow Girl.

He moves slowly at first, drawing out every thrust, making her arch her back and groan every time he pulls out.

Gregory holds her open and is watching his cock disappear into her, watching her stretch to take him. He pumps like this for a few minutes low and deep, before sliding one hand down, making her whimper when he takes her clit and rubs as he fucks her harder.

I get to my feet, undo the top buttons of my shirt, adjust my pants. I go to her, lean down, cup the back of her head and pet her.

Her breathing is ragged and sweat has collected on her forehead and I smile down at her. "Remember, sweetheart, don't come."

"It's not fair," she blurts out and squeezes her eyes closed when Greg smacks her ass.

I straighten, take in the sight of him fucking her, of his dick stretching her, one hand holding her spread, the thumb of that hand now circling her asshole.

"Not her ass," I say. That's mine.

He looks at me, nods, and I shift my gaze to her face again, and I hear the familiar sound she makes when she's coming. She's coming on my brother's dick and he fucks her harder for it and in another moment, he's coming too, thrusting deep into her, emptying inside her, filling up my Willow Girl.

"I'm sorry," she starts, looking up at me. "I'm sorry."

I lay my hand on her head, lay her cheek down.

Gregory pulls out, tucks his dick into his briefs and closes his pants. We both watch as cum drips out of her cunt and down her thighs and fuck, I'm fucking hard.

"I'm sorry," she tries again.

I look up at Greg, then at her.

"What are we going to do with you, Willow Girl?"

14

HELENA

I remain as I am, bent over the table, naked from the waist down, and almost so from the waist up. I feel cum dripping down my thighs as they stand behind me watching.

"It wasn't really fair," I try, not looking back, knowing it doesn't matter. He knew I'd come.

"Shh." Sebastian sits back down. "Stay," he tells me.

Greg picks up his drink and follows him to sit and takes a sip.

"I feel responsible," he says to Sebastian.

He's got his back to me, but I can almost hear the smug grin in his voice.

"It wasn't fair," I try again from my place at the table, the night breeze cool on my naked ass.

"Life isn't fair," Gregory says.

"How are you going to punish me?"

"I'm going to leave that up to my brother," Sebastian says.

Gregory turns to me with a grin on his face. "I'll think of something special."

My glare is interrupted by Sebastian's command. "Go to your room, Helena."

I'm surprised by this and a little put off at being sent away like a child.

"Go. I need to talk to my brother alone."

I look at the both of them and I guess I should be grateful he's letting me go. Although a look at Gregory tells me my punishment won't be forgotten.

Without a word, I go to leave.

"Helena," Sebastian says, stopping me when I get to the door.

I turn.

"Be ready for me when I get up there."

I bite my lip, nod, and go upstairs. I didn't really think he wasn't going to fuck me tonight, did I? And honestly, don't I want him to?

First thing I do is have a shower, taking my time. Before getting into bed, I retrieve Aunt Helena's journal from beneath the mattress and re-read those final passages.

When I get the chance, I'm going to have to go back to the mausoleum and see if I can find the door that leads to the room below. I don't know what I'll find, don't know why it matters, but it does.

I tuck it away in its hiding place and lay on my

side, pulling the blanket over myself and closing my eyes. I don't turn out the lights. I haven't since I've been back from that dark room, not when I'm alone.

When I wake, it's because of the sudden cold as my comforter is pulled from me.

I open my eyes to find Sebastian standing over me. He's still fully dressed and he takes in my naked body.

"Did you leave the lights on on purpose?"

"I can't sleep if it's dark anymore. Not when I'm alone, at least."

He nods, pulls his shirt over his head. I look at the scar.

"That must have hurt," I say.

He looks at it too, then back at me. "It's nothing."

I sit up. "What did Gregory say to you in Gallo's office? He said something in Italian that made you stop. What was it?"

He sighs, turns his attention to stripping off the rest of his clothes. "Nothing that matters."

"It looked like it mattered."

"Did it?" he asks, closing his hand over my ankle and tugging me to lie flat on the bed before spinning me onto my belly and pulling me toward him. "This is what matters right now," he says.

I look back to find him kneeling between my legs beside the bed as he wraps his arms around my thighs and forces my back to arch. He looks at me like that, spread and open for him.

"Did you clean my brother's cum out of you?"

I flush, but nod.

"Do you like getting fucked by him while I watch?" he asks, dipping his head to lick my pussy.

I bite my lip, grip the sheets.

"Do you?"

"Yes."

"You're a dirty girl, Helena," he says, licking me in slow, long stretches, teasing my clit, making me want.

He stands up, puts his hands on my ass and spreads me open, touches a finger to my asshole. "This is mine," he says as he draws me up to my knees.

I look back at him. He's not looking at my face though.

"No one fucks your ass but me."

"Why do you share me with him? It bothers you."

"Does it bother you?"

I think about this. "I don't know. I thought it would."

"We shared girls before. Done it a few times. It was easier then."

"Easier to share?"

He nods.

"Then don't do it. Don't share me with him."

He holds my gaze as he pushes his cock into me. It's too fast, and I'm not ready. It hurts a little.

"I like looking at you when you take him."

He thrusts again.

"Are you always going to punish me after you make me fuck him?" Because that is what he's doing. He's punishing me now.

"After I *make* you? I think you like it."

I pull away. I only manage it because he's not expecting me to. I get off the bed, stand almost nose to nose with him.

"Don't put this on me. You own me, remember? And you told him to fuck me."

I don't know why I'm so angry all of a sudden. Maybe it's because there's truth to his words? Maybe it's because I do want it.

I like having them both. I do. But at the same time, Sebastian sharing me with his brother, it leaves a space between us. A barrier. And this makes no sense to me. It's what I thought before. What I felt. When we were in Verona and he talked to me like he did. When he made love to me. I couldn't take that because what I was feeling, what I *am* feeling, I cannot feel for him.

I think about my Aunt Helena, remember what I read in her journal. She was in love with one too.

In love with one.

What is wrong with me? What's wrong with us Willow Girls?

"Get back on the bed, Helena."

"I don't feel like a fuck." I shake my head, still in

my thoughts, and walk around him, but he captures my arm, stops me.

"I said get on the bed. All fours. Ass to me."

I try to tug free. "I'm not in the mood."

"Suddenly not in the mood?" he asks, taking both my arms now and backing me into the wall. "You were in the mood earlier," he says, shoving me roughly against it.

"Stop."

He lifts me up, lifts one thigh over his waist and impales me on his cock.

The roses embossed on the wallpaper press their pattern into my back.

"You were in the mood to fuck my brother but not me?" He thrusts again. He has one hand around my hip, digging fingers into my skin, and with the other, he's holding my wrist to the wall above my head while I cling to him with my free arm.

"You told him to fuck me. You said you wanted to watch."

"And you got off on it, just like you'll get off now. Because your pussy's wet enough." His eyes are locked on mine as he thrusts in fast and hard and deep.

"What's your problem?" I ask through shortened breaths while I cling to him. "You want it, you want to watch me get fucked by him, you set some ridiculous rule that I can't come. You even give him permission to punish me. What does that even mean?"

"Shut up, Helena."

"No, Sebastian, because if you own me, you own this too. You own what happens to me."

"I said shut up."

He tries to kiss my mouth, but I turn my face away and he ends up mashing his mouth against my cheek.

"You know what I think?" I start.

He releases my wrist and grips my jaw instead, makes me look at him.

"What do you think?"

I can hear us, hear the wet sounds of fucking, my resolve fading.

I'm going to come soon.

Anger transforms into sadness that settles inside my belly.

"I think there's something wrong with us Willow Girls," I say quietly.

He shifts his grip to cup my ass and, with his cock still deep inside me, he carries me to the bed and lays me down. He stands at the edge of it and pushes my knees up to fuck me deep, bringing his face close to mine.

"What's wrong with you Willow Girls?" he asks.

I'm clinging to him, my hands on his shoulders and neck. I dig my nails into his skin, into his scar.

He winces. I know it hurts him, but I also know he gets off on it.

"That we want it. Like this. That *I* want you. Still. After everything, I want you."

He kisses my mouth and I open to him and I feel my fingernails break skin, feel the warmth of blood on my fingertips.

"Fuck, Helena."

"I think we all have this sickness. The Willow Girl sickness."

He draws back a little and I wrap my hand around the back of his head and pull him closer, kiss him hard, use my teeth. His cock grows thicker inside me.

He shoves my legs wider and I fist his short hair, tug to hurt because I'm coming. I'm coming again, and he feels me and he's watching me.

We're both sick, I guess. Our families are sick.

He fists a handful of my hair and forces me to look at him and I hear myself moan, and his cock feels so good.

I ride the orgasm to its last, and he's still fucking me, still watching me.

"No matter what," I say, taking his final thrusts as he begins to throb inside me, filling me up, bruising me inside and out. "No matter what, we *want* the Scafoni bastards."

15

HELENA

After breakfast the next morning, I get the chance to slip away. Sebastian is in his study with the door closed and Gregory's off the island. I take Lucinda's letter opener with me as I head to the mausoleum. I tell myself it's just in case I need to pick a lock.

I take the same path as last time except that today, I'm wearing jeans, a sweater and sneakers so even though it's warm, my arms and legs are protected.

The same feeling passes over me as I near the dark, gray building, and I only allow myself to slow my steps when I meet the angel's watchful eye.

I give her the finger and stand up straighter as I push the gate open and enter.

The sudden cold makes me shudder. I hate it here.

The red lantern burns and the way the sunlight inches in, the space is almost creepier today.

But I don't have to be here long.

I just need to find that door and go downstairs—which is sure to be even more creepy—and find out what they did to Aunt Helena. Find out what she thought would free her even though she was terrified of whatever it was.

At first sight, I don't see it. It takes me two full turns around the place to realize there's a small opening between two of the walls. It's narrow and covered over with cobwebs.

I pull my sweater down into my hand and sweep them away and nearly jump when I feel what I am sure is a spider scurry across the back of my hand. I peek into the dark space, but this can't be anything. It's too narrow. I could barely fit through myself. No way a man could slip through here. Neither Sebastian nor Gregory could.

I shake my head, wipe off the cobwebs step outside into the sunlight to rethink this. I take a deep breath in through my nose, realizing I only breathe in gasps when I'm in there. It's like you can taste the dead.

The angel is still watching, but I swear she's mocking me now.

That's when I notice the path around the mausoleum. It's overgrown with weeds which explains why I haven't seen it before.

I begin the walk around the building, studying the walls. I don't know why I'm expecting some hidden entrance or secret door or something because almost at the very back of the building is another entrance, gates like the ones at the front. It's not hidden at all. There's a heavy, rusted chain weaving through the bars, but the lock is hanging open.

Rust flakes when I touch it, pull the chain through the bars, trying to make as little noise as possible, but making too much. I'm far enough from the house that they shouldn't hear, though, and it doesn't take too long because it looks like someone's been here recently.

Once I have it loose, I push the gate open. It creaks even louder than those at the main entrance and stone stairs lead straight down into blackness.

I take a step down and feel in my pocket for the letter opener and keep telling myself ghosts aren't real even though I know they are.

The ring on my finger burns. I swear it's searing itself into my skin.

Maybe it's Cain Scafoni.

Maybe he wants his finger back.

The thought gives me strength and I take another step.

The smell of decay is strong here. It's just leaves though, and earth and damp. Not that I've ever smelled decaying human bodies, although I imagine that must be worse.

But I can't go too much farther. It's not practical. At least that's what I tell myself.

I'll need a flashlight. It's pitch black.

When I turn, I run back up the uneven stairs, tripping once and smashing my knee against unforgiving stone, hurrying, ignoring the pain, because all of a sudden, it's like when I was a kid at home and my sisters and I would dare each other to go down to the old cellar—it was off limits to us—and I was the only one ever brave enough to do it. I remember running back up once I was all the way down and swearing I felt something try to grab at my ankles, try to drag me down into the darkness.

I shudder at the memory.

I'm sure it's my imagination but that's how I feel now, and my heart is racing by the time I get back outside in the sun, on the dead grass.

As quickly as I can, I shove the gate closed and weave the chain through it and run back around to the path that will lead me away from here. Away from this haunted place even though I know I'll have to come back.

My breath is just back to normal when I near the house, but when I find Gregory leaning against the wall watching me, my heart starts to pound again.

"I thought you were gone," I say as casually as possible, not looking at him as I try to slip past into the house because I'm sure he can see the guilt on my face.

He grabs my wrist, stops me. I look at where he's looking then watch him pick off some of the cobwebs still clinging to my sleeve.

"Where were you, Willow Girl?" he asks, looking down over me, down at where my jeans must have torn when I stumbled on the stairs. I didn't realize my knee was bleeding.

I clear my throat, try to hold his gaze. "I fell." It's true.

"I see that. Where did you fall?"

"Oh, just out and about. On the grounds." Of course, I'd be on the grounds. Where else? It's an island and I need to shut up.

He raises his eyebrows.

"I'd better go change. Put a bandage on my knee."

He nods. No way he believes that I've just been *out and about*.

I take a step away.

"I'll help," he says.

He falls into step with me and I stop to look up at him. "What?"

"I'll help."

"Why?"

He looks down at me, smiles a smile that says he's up to something—as if I didn't know—and gestures for me to go up the stairs ahead of him.

I go, and once I'm in my room, he closes the door and looks at me.

"Pants off so we can get a look at that knee."

"I'm perfectly capable of—"

"Relax, Helena, I'm just fucking with you. I actually came to give you something."

"Give me something?"

He steps toward me. "Well, more like loan it to you." He reaches into his pocket and, to my surprise, takes out a cell phone. He holds it out to me.

I look cautiously on. I'm sure he's still fucking with me.

"What's that for?" I ask.

"Thought you'd want to call home. You haven't talked to your family since you've been here."

I'm almost salivating at the prospect, but with him, I know to be cautious.

"But if you don't want to..." He starts to put it away.

"Wait."

He looks up at me, gives me a grin. Raises an eyebrow.

"What's the catch?"

"You're not a very trusting person, are you, Helena?"

I shift my weight to one foot and set my hands on my hips. "I know you, Gregory."

"You *think* you know me, Helena."

"What's the catch?" I repeat.

He holds the phone out to me. "No catch. You've got ten minutes. Oh, wait, one thing. I don't want you calling a boyfriend."

"I don't have a boyfriend and you know it." I take it from him, taking care not to touch skin to skin. "Why are you doing this?"

"Why not?" he asks, but when I think he's going to leave to give me privacy, he instead parks himself on my bed, stretches out his legs, puts his hands behind his head and starts to whistle some tune.

I open my mouth but as if he expects what I'm going to say, he speaks first.

"Beggars can't be choosers, Helena." He checks his watch. "Nine minutes."

I go into the bathroom and close the door. I don't have to think about who I'm going to call.

I have no interest in wasting my time by calling my parents. Instead, sitting on the edge of the tub, I dial Amy, my youngest sister. I've almost given up hope when, on the fifth ring, just before the call goes to voicemail, she picks up.

My eyes well up at the familiar sound of her voice and I can't speak right away. It takes her two times of asking who it is for me to answer.

"It's me, Amy. It's Helena."

"Helena?"

Tears stream down my face and I'm nodding like an idiot. "Yes. It's me."

"Helena. Oh my God, Helena! I didn't think I'd

hear from you." She pauses. "Not while you were...there."

"Oh, Amy it's so good to just hear your voice. How are you?"

She pauses. "Helena, you know about...you received my letter?"

"The obituary. Yes." I nod to no one. "Yes, I know. I didn't find out until two weeks later, but I know now."

"I wish I could have called."

"It's okay. It's okay, Amy. I'm grateful you sent the letter."

There's an awkward silence.

"How is he?" she finally asks. "How are they?"

"He's okay." I leave the 'they' out.

"Are they...hurting you?"

"I'm okay. Sebastian is okay."

"I know why they did it. Why mom and dad did this, I mean. They told me, finally, after they were fed up of me. I know where the money is coming from. I know why we're making repairs on the house. Why dad bought a new car."

Hearing this, I want to cry. This is what my life is worth.

Things.

Material things.

"I've even been enrolled at St. Joe's."

"Oh, Amy, that's great." My heart is sinking and the optimism in my voice is forced. She must hear it.

"No, Helena, it's not. You're paying for it with...with...skin."

I can't help the sniffle and she hears it.

"I'm leaving. I won't be part of this," she says.

"It could as easily have been you, Amy."

"And you'd have stayed? Knowing the truth?"

"No." I don't need to think about my answer. I know I wouldn't.

"Besides, I knew it would be you. The instant he saw you, I knew it. It was in his eyes. It was only ever you, Helena."

Why does her saying that make me stop?

A knock on my door and Gregory peeks his head in, taps his watch, and I'm back in the present.

"I don't have much time to talk, Amy."

"You have to go?"

I nod even though I know she can't see it. "Just please don't do anything rash. Take the money and go to school. You'll still be away from the house, from them. It's important. You have to think about your future."

"I can't do that, Helena. Besides, what about your future? What happens to you after? The same thing that happened to Aunt Libby or even Aunt Helena?"

"Aunt Helena was fine."

"She wasn't fine. Not really."

I think about what Sebastian said about her, how she wasn't all there, not by the end. I think about what happened to her. About the ring on my finger.

"What will you do otherwise, Amy, if you don't go to school?"

"Live with integrity. Besides, I didn't say I wouldn't go to school. I just won't go on these terms. It's blood money, Helena, no matter how okay you say he is to you." I hear her sniffle and I know she's trying to hide her tears.

Gregory steps into the room now. "Time."

"Amy," I start.

Gregory holds out his hand.

"Can I call you again?" she asks. "I'll store the number."

I look at up Gregory and I realize the catch. He'll now have access to the one person I chose to call, the one sister I'm close with.

And maybe he'll decide to take his own Willow Girl.

"Delete it, Amy. And block it. I'll find another way to call you."

Gregory watches me, his expression unreadable. Not angry, just level.

"Helena—"

But she's cut off because he takes the phone and disconnects. He tucks it into his pocket.

"Who's Amy?"

I try to grab the phone back. "Give me that." I want to delete his history, delete her number. Not that it matters. He knows it's Amy. He'll find some way to get access to her if that's what he wants.

He catches my arm easily.

"What do you think I'm going to do with the number exactly? Call her? Ask her out on a date? Or are you afraid I'll take my own Willow Girl maybe?"

"She's not yours. You can't touch her. I'll kill you if you touch her!"

"Kill me?" He pauses, feigns being hurt. "I was only doing you a kindness. I won't make that mistake again." He turns to go.

"Wait."

He stops.

"I am grateful. I just..."

He turns back to me.

"You're not going to do anything to her." I don't know if it's a question or a statement of fact or what.

"I'm glad you could talk to her, Helena," he says rather than answering my question.

"Can I call her again soon?"

"We'll see. Go get that cleaned up."

With that, he walks out of my room and I'm left watching the door, confused by his motives, worried for my sister, not liking this new secret between Gregory and myself.

16

SEBASTIAN

"You're chipper," I say to Gregory as he digs into his second serving of pasta.

"I'm always chipper," he says. "You're the broody one. You should lighten up, brother."

He's normally about as chipper as Lucinda, and Helena is quieter than usual, studying my brother whenever he isn't studying her. I can almost see the gears of her mind working.

"What did you do today, Helena?"

Gregory takes his last bite of food, lays his utensils diagonally across his plate and sits back, wiping his mouth and watching Helena.

"Just walked a little. Swam and read."

"How's your knee?" Gregory asks.

Helena flushes. "It's fine."

"What happened to your knee?" I ask.

"Nothing. I just fell and scraped it up. It looked

worse than it was when you saw it," she says, directing the last part at Greg.

"How's your sister?" I ask.

Helena coughs, choking on the bite she was just swallowing, and drops her fork. She covers her mouth with her napkin.

When the coughing fit passes, she pushes her chair back to pick up the fork.

"Leave it," I say.

She straightens as a girl comes to replace her fork with a new one.

I take my time swallowing my food. What did I expect from this test? Did I think she'd tell me? No. I didn't. Maybe I hoped she would. But this is more than that.

I glance to my brother who's watching her. I don't like how he watches her, but I have to be careful and measured.

Helena's waiting for my reaction. I chew on another bite of food before focusing my gaze on her.

"That call must have been a more pivotal part of your day than your walk. Did it slip your mind?"

She shifts her gaze to Gregory then back to me. "You knew?"

"I asked Gregory to give you the phone to make the call," I answer her.

"Was it a test?" she asks.

I shrug a shoulder.

"Just for me or for him too?"

"Oh, it was for me too, Helena. Have no doubt," Gregory says.

Helena pushes her chair back. Stands. "Well, then I guess I owe you a thanks."

"Sit down."

"I'm done. I don't like being played with."

She walks past my chair, but I grab hold of her wrist and push my chair back to tug her down onto my lap.

Gregory gets up, disappears inside for a moment, I assume to dismiss the staff. He returns and resumes his seat, smiling wide.

I keep Helena's wrists in my hands behind her.

"When I say sit, you sit," I tell her.

She doesn't say anything back but squirms a little. She won't be moving away, not until I allow it. She knows it, too. And I know in a fucked-up kind of way, she likes it. I wonder if there's security in it for her. I wonder if she knows, maybe on a subconscious level, that she's safe with me, even when I punish her.

"What did Amy have to say?" I ask at her neck.

Gregory crosses one ankle over his other knee and drinks the last of his wine. He gives Helena a wink.

"Why didn't you tell me you were just being your brother's errand boy?" she asks him.

I see him chafe at that.

"You didn't ask," he says through gritted teeth.

"What did Amy say?" I ask again. I'll let them hash that other part out later. That was part of the point of this exercise, after all.

"My parents told her about the money. They enrolled her in school."

"What else?"

"She's leaving home. She won't accept the money."

"Why not?"

"Because she has integrity, Sebastian," Helena snaps, turning her head just enough to see me from the corner of one eye. "Something that the Scafoni brothers lack. I don't like being played with."

"Then learn to be honest. Know that I know everything that happens here, whether you think I do or not. You won't come between my brother and I."

"It's not my intention to. It never has been."

But it's happening. There's already a small fissure between us that I fear is only the beginning.

I meet Gregory's gaze and I know that in time, if we follow the rules, I'll have to give her to him. She'll belong to him.

The thought makes my insides burn and I need to manage this, and this is the only way.

Swapping her wrists into one of my hands, I draw the zipper of her dress down.

She makes a sound, a small whimper, but remains as she is as I slide one sleeve, then the other off her shoulders and to the crease of her elbows. I then do the same with the straps of her bra then unhook it, let it slip down to expose her breasts.

Gregory's eyes momentarily shift down to take them in before returning to hers.

"Stand up," I say.

I keep hold of her when she does and nod to Gregory who reaches forward, slides his hands up along her legs to grip her panties and drag them down and off. Then, swapping my grip, I let the dress and bra fall to the floor before seating her naked on my lap again.

Gregory looks her over.

"Spread your legs for my brother."

It takes a nudge from me, but she does it, shifting them as wide as mine, only the balls of her feet on the floor.

Gregory looks at the seam of her sex as she squirms. I don't stop him when he leans forward, rubs her pussy with two fingers, then smears them on her thigh.

"I think she likes this," he says.

"I think you're right. I smell her arousal from here," I say, leaning in close to her ear before standing her up, handing her over to my brother.

He takes hold of her wrists, keeps them at her sides, kisses her belly, kisses lower, before turning her, handing her back to me.

I take her nipple into my mouth before drawing

back, dragging it between my teeth until she whimpers.

Greg stands, shoves the plates out of the way, sending one crashing in his haste. He lifts her, sits her on the edge of the table and leans in close to her so she has to lean back. He pulls his shirt over his head and grips her legs, widening them, standing between them.

I can see he wants to kiss her. He's so close, so close.

But he kisses her neck instead, then lower, the hollow of her collarbone, her chest, between her breasts, the oval of her belly button. He's on his knees, hands on her thighs as he leans in to lick her pussy, tasting her as she squeezes her eyes closed and leans farther back.

I watch at first, watch her struggle.

She puts her hands on his head, trying to push him off as she turns to me.

"Is this another test?"

She shoves at him, but he grabs her wrists, pulls them apart.

She fists her hands, puts one foot on the table intending to scoot away, but ends up opening her legs wider instead.

"Please!"

"Brother," I say, eyes locked on her desperate ones.

He pulls back, stands, wipes his mouth. He sits

down on his chair, undoes his jeans, shoves them down and fists his cock.

I stand up, take Helena by the arm and pull her off the table.

"What are you doing?" she asks in a whisper.

I cup her cheek in one hand.

"What are *we* doing?" she asks.

I have to keep control of this, of him. Of her. This is the only way. It's the only way to keep her mine.

And as much as I don't want to, I turn her around and set her on her knees before my brother.

"Suck him off, Helena."

She doesn't turn back, but hesitates, and it takes Gregory's hand on the back of her head for her to take him into her mouth.

I kneel behind her, pull off my shirt, undo my pants. Gripping her ass, I splay her open and when I feel her, I feel how wet she is.

As much as she fights this, she wants it too and part of me, it wants to punish her for it. To hate her for it. But I don't.

Instead, I slide into her wet cunt and lean forward over her back.

"Now you can come, but make sure when my brother does, that you swallow every drop. Not one wasted. Understand?"

She nods, and I straighten, looking down at her, her pretty, wet cunt stretched wide with me inside her, her little asshole so inviting.

Greg grips a handful of hair and begins to fuck her face and when he does, I match his thrusts, hard and fast and deep and in moments, she's coming, and the throbbing of her pussy takes me over the edge and I fill up her cunt as my brother empties down her throat and for a single moment, I let myself believe this can work.

The three of us.

Like this.

As long as she's mine to give.

Mine to share.

Mine to keep.

But as the bliss of orgasm retreats, that fantasy fades.

I know in my bones that this won't end well.

That this Willow Girl will destroy my brother and me both.

17

HELENA

I sleep alone that night. I go to my room afterwards and take a long shower and I don't know why, but I cry a little.

I don't understand why Sebastian did what he did. Testing me with that call. Sharing me.

And I'm worried about Amy.

This whole thing, it's fucked up and it just keeps getting more and more fucked up.

Late the next afternoon, Gregory seeks me out in my room. I haven't seen Sebastian all day.

"Come with me, Willow Girl."

"I'm not going anywhere with you."

"You don't have a choice."

"What, you have another test for me? You and your brother cook one up last night?"

He takes a deep breath in and exhales. "This isn't a test."

"Yeah, well I don't exactly trust you."

"That's not new. Come on."

"Why?"

"You're owed a punishment, remember?"

I feel my face go white.

"Relax, Helena. I'm not going to hurt you." He sits on the edge of the bed. "I just want some company, okay?"

The way he looks at me, there's something in his eyes that is so wounded. So much like a lost little puppy and it gets me every fucking time.

Why does this always weaken me?

He continues. I know he reads my face. "You spend a few hours with me and you can consider yourself absolved. Almost painless, apart from having to endure my company."

"A few hours doing what?"

"You'll see. I promise you'll enjoy it." He smiles what I want to believe is a genuine smile. "I'll give you five minutes," he says and walks away. "Wear a bikini. It may be one of the last days of swimming weather."

He leaves, and I reluctantly change into a bikini. I put on shorts and a light sweater on top. I wonder if Sebastian knows about Gregory's plan for my punishment, and I don't know why but I believe him when he says this isn't a test.

Gregory checks his watch when I get downstairs. "Prompt."

"Does Sebastian know about this?"

"Don't worry about my brother. Let's go."

"Where are we going?" I ask as I follow him toward the far end of the beach.

He doesn't reply until we get to our destination and I see it.

"Canoe ride."

I stop.

The canoe looks like it hasn't been used in years. I wonder if this is the one Sebastian took out that day he tipped it. The day he almost killed Ethan.

From the look on Gregory's face, he knows what I'm thinking. I wonder if Sebastian told him the story of what truly happened that day out there.

I watch as he shoves dead branches and leaves off and rights it, seeing the muscles on his arms and back flex as he works.

When he turns back to me, I flush.

"Is it safe?" I ask to distract him or myself, I'm not sure which.

"You're a strong swimmer," he says, not quite answering my question as he drags it out to the water.

He takes off his flip flops and tosses them into the canoe. He's wearing shorts and a T-shirt and walks into the water, dragging it behind him.

"Gregory are you sure it's safe?"

"Don't worry," he says, looking back at me. "I won't tip it."

He knows about Ethan. He must know. Is he testing whether or not I know? Why does it matter? Maybe he doesn't like that his brother told me?

I sigh, take off my flip flops and follow him into the turquoise sea.

The water is cool on my feet and ankles and I toss my flip flops into the canoe too. Once we're a little farther, he stops and gestures for me to get in.

Reluctantly, I do.

He pulls us out a little farther before climbing in himself and picking up the oar to row us out.

"It's beautiful out here," he says. "Peaceful."

It is. The only sound is the breeze and water calmly lapping up against the canoe.

"Do you come out here a lot?" I ask, dropping one hand out to dip my fingers into the water. We're sitting facing each other, the island at my back.

"Not really."

"Why did we come today?"

"There's a little cove where you can swim. I thought you might like that."

I study him. I don't believe he's just doing this for me. When it comes to the three of us, Gregory has an agenda.

But then again, so does Sebastian. Wasn't yesterday proof of that?

"Does Sebastian know?"

"Sure."

"Oh."

He rows in silence and I look around, feeling awkward but trying to relax. To enjoy the beauty of it. Besides, maybe he's genuine. Maybe I need to listen to myself, to what I told Sebastian, that Gregory's lonely. That's all.

"Where did you take your tumble yesterday?" he asks, looking at my scraped-up knee.

I shrug a shoulder. "Nowhere special. I just tripped over a rock."

He nods. "And there were cobwebs around?"

"I guess I fell into a spiderweb."

"Right."

I want to change the subject. "How far to the cove?"

"Not far."

"Why didn't you tell me Sebastian arranged for me to call my sister? Why set me up?"

"Did you ever consider it was him setting you up? Or maybe setting us up?"

"Why would he?"

"Because he can."

"You both can. I'm stuck in the middle and it's not where I want to be."

"No? Because I get the feeling you like it just fine when you're between us."

I look away. I know he means the sex and I can't deny what he's saying, but that part, it's different.

"Maybe it was his way to make sure you don't trust me," he says.

"I don't trust you."

I see an infinitesimal change in his eyes, a moment of vulnerability almost. Although it's gone in an instant and maybe it wasn't there at all. Maybe it was my imagination.

I clear my throat. "What did you say to Sebastian that night in Gallo's office? You said something in Italian I couldn't understand."

"You should ask him."

"I did. He wouldn't tell me."

"Maybe there's a reason for that. Besides, it's not my place to tell you."

"Your place?"

"You're *his* Willow Girl, remember? You both keep reminding me of that. As if I'd forget."

I study him, try to figure out what he's thinking, what he's planning.

"Whose canoe is this?"

"Sebastian's."

I knew that already, didn't I?

"He hasn't taken it out since the accident. He told you about that?"

I nod.

"He trusts you. Are you trustworthy, Helena?"

"What do you want, Gregory? What's this about?"

He shrugs a shoulder, gestures behind me.

I turn to find we're approaching a small island or more like a big rock. I watch as he rows us to it, and as we come around the wall of rock, I see the small, pretty, sand beach hidden there.

He rows closer, as close as we can before climbing out, and he drags the canoe onto the sand.

"I didn't know there was anything like this here," I say.

He sits on the sand and pats the space beside him.

"Does Sebastian know we're here?" I ask again.

"Don't worry about my brother." Same answer.

"What do you want? Why did you bring me here?"

"You never answered my question from the other night."

"You don't answer any of mine."

"Okay, one for one. I'll even go first. Ask me a question."

"Really?"

"Yes."

"What did you say to Sebastian?"

"I told him he knew the way out."

"The way out?"

He nods.

"Way out of this, you mean?"

"That's two questions."

"Not really—"

"My turn."

"Wait, that's not really fair. You can't just—"

"Told you the other night that life isn't fair. How

have you not figured that out yet? You of all people, Willow Girl?"

I look out toward the water. "I'm going to swim." I don't wait for permission and I'm fully aware he won't forget to ask his question, but at least I can buy some time.

I strip off my shorts and sweater and walk out into the water. He doesn't follow but I feel him watching me as I dip beneath the surface and swim out away from the island. I open my eyes beneath the water. It's crystal clear here but the salt stings my eyes, and although it's shallow right here, it gets deep fast. Pretty silvery-white fish swim away as I approach, and I wish I had goggles. Maybe I'll ask Sebastian to bring me back to snorkel.

I'm floating on my back on the water, eyes closed. My ears are beneath the surface which is why I don't hear him until he's so close, he's touching me.

I startle, go under in my panic.

He wraps an arm around my middle and brings me to the surface.

I suck in a breath, push the hair back from my face.

"I'm fine! I can swim just fine!"

But he doesn't let me go. He keeps his arm locked around me.

"My question," he says.

I look up at him, see how the turquoise of the sea lights up those specks in his eyes.

"What about how you look at me?" he asks.

I know what he's talking about. It was just as he'd asked me this question at Gallo's that we were interrupted.

But I don't want to answer it, so I shove at him and slip out from under his arm, swimming back to the beach, away from him.

But he's beside me in a moment and there's nowhere to go and when I sit on the sand he sits down beside me.

"You made a deal. I answered your question."

"That's debatable."

"Now it's your turn."

I look at him but before I can speak, he does.

"I want to kiss you, Helena," he says. He reaches out to push hair that's stuck to my face back. "He lets me lick your pussy. Lets me fuck you. But I can't kiss you and I so badly want to kiss you."

I shake my head no, pull my knees in.

"Just a kiss. That's all."

I shake my head again and keep my gaze over the water.

He puts his hand on my cheek, turns me to look at him. "Because you don't want to or because you're scared of him?"

"I'm not scared of him."

"Then you don't want to."

"Why are you doing this? Another test?"

"No test. I give you my word. Answer my question. What about how you look at me?"

"What did you expect? That you'd bring me here and I'd...I'd...what?" I start to get up, but he catches my wrist, stopping me.

"Answer my question, Helena."

"Why? Why is this important?"

"It is important. It's important to me."

"I don't love you," the words are out before I can think about them or process what I'm saying myself.

They silence him.

They silence us both.

I hear what I've just said.

When he finally speaks, his tone is different. Hard. "Do you love *him*?" he asks through gritted teeth.

"I want to go back."

"Answer me."

"You get one question just like I did."

He studies me and hurt wars with rage and I know the latter is winning from the way his eyes darken.

"I want to go back to the island. Now." I stand.

He gets to his feet. "You know he almost killed his brother, don't you?"

"It was an accident."

"You don't believe that."

I stop, look down at the ground. No, I know it's not true. I know it wasn't an accident.

I shake my head no and look up at him. "I know what really happened, but I also know he was a child."

"Sixteen isn't a child. Not in our family."

"What's your problem? He loves you. And I defended you to him."

"I don't need you to defend me. That's not what you're for. But don't worry, you'll be safe from me. If he has the balls to go through with it."

"Go through with what?" My aunt's journal comes to mind, the marking ceremony.

He walks away. "I'll take you back to the island like you want, Helena."

"Goes through with what, Gregory?" I ask again, refusing to move.

He comes back, takes my arm, leans in close. "Maybe you don't want to know, Willow Girl." He drags me to the canoe, picking up our discarded clothes on the way and tossing them into it.

"Get in."

"I didn't mean to hurt you."

"You didn't hurt me. Get in."

"Gregory—"

"Get in the fucking boat before I leave you here!"

I jump at his tone and I climb into the canoe and he pushes it out, then climbs in himself and begins to row us back to the island, not speaking a word, his eyes burning a hole into me.

18

SEBASTIAN

I'm lying on Helena's bed reading when she walks into the room. She startles, stops.

Her hair's wet and she's wearing a bikini, carrying her clothes. She's out of breath.

"Where were you?" I ask.

Her eyes fall on the notebook I'm reading. "What are you doing?" She comes forward, goes to grab it out of my hands.

I pull it away, stand up. "Maid found it tucked between the mattress and the box spring when she was changing the sheets. How long have you had this?"

"It doesn't matter. It's none of your business."

"Well, actually, yes, it is my business."

She rubs her hand over her forehead. "I can't deal with this right now." She goes into the bathroom, closes the door.

I open it. She's standing at the sink, the clothes she was holding in a heap on the floor. She's looking at her reflection but I'm not sure she's seeing anything at all.

"Mind telling me what the fuck is going on?"

She turns the taps, washes her face. "I need a shower."

"Why?"

"Because your brother just took me out to some island for a swim and I'm salty from the water. All right?"

"What island?"

"A cove. Not an island."

I feel my jaw tighten. "What did he do?"

"Nothing."

"Doesn't look like it was nothing."

"Just leave it alone."

I go to the sink, switch the taps off. "Did he touch you?"

She looks at me. "It's always the same thing. You let him touch me, Sebastian. Remember? More than once."

"And I remember you liking it," I say, grabbing her arms, shaking her. "I remember hearing you come. Can't get the sound out of my head, in fact."

"You know what? I did like it, I liked him fucking me. I came. And maybe I should have let him do what he wanted—"

"What did he want?"

"To kiss me. Just to kiss me. That's all."

I release her and when she walks back into the bedroom, I follow her.

"Kissing is different. Intimate," I say.

"How is fucking less intimate? I mean, I get it that he's confused. You put me out there and then you take me back. Hang me back out there, then snatch me back. And I can't tell what you want. What you're doing out of obligation." She drops to a seat on the bed. "I can't even tell what I want."

I stand back, watch her. "I control it. He can only touch you when I say. He can only touch you how I say. I control it."

"But you can't control emotions, Sebastian. It doesn't work that way, not even for you. You can try to arrange us the way you want in your stupid game and you still can't control what we feel. No one can!"

"Get showered and changed and stay in your room. I need to have a word with my brother."

She looks up at me. "What are you going to do?"

"That'll be between me and him."

"You have so many secrets, so much *between you and him*. So how come I'm always the one in the middle? How come I'm always the one tugged around, stretched to the point of breaking?"

I take a minute to answer. I know this broken record.

"It's what happens. What the Willow Girl does." I walk to the door but stop and turn back. "Here too,"

I say, holding up the notebook. "With your aunt. Only then with extreme consequences. I won't let that happen to my brother and me."

"You want it all. You want me. You want him. It's not going to work. Don't you see that? Someone's going to get hurt. Maybe all of us."

Fuck.

I run a hand through my hair.

"I need to find my brother."

She shakes her head, turns away.

I walk out the door, down the stairs. I drop the book on my desk before heading out of the house and I find my brother exactly where I think I'll find him.

"What the fuck did you think you were doing taking that thing out? Taking her in it?" I ask.

Gregory's sitting on top of the upside-down canoe smoking a cigarette. He's stored it back where I'd left it that day years ago. The last time I took it out.

He takes the last drag on his cigarette before dropping it to the ground, burying it in the sand. He stands, looks at me.

"Don't worry about it," he says, walking toward me, then past me. "She's back, safe and sound. *I* didn't tip the canoe."

I grab his arm, stop him. "What the fuck does that mean?"

"Please. I'm not fucking stupid. Ethan wasn't ever

a good swimmer and you knew it. You wanted to punish Lucinda? What did you do instead? You destroyed any chance of Ethan having a normal life."

"Like you give a shit about him."

"He didn't deserve what he got."

Fuck. He's right. "I didn't...It wasn't like that."

"No? How was it?"

I release him, look out toward the water, run a hand through my hair. "What I did to Ethan," I start through clenched teeth, "it was a mistake. One I've paid for."

At that he chuckles. "You paid? How did you pay exactly?"

I follow him with my eyes as he turns a circle around me.

"Because from where I stand, only one person paid and that was Ethan," he says. "And he doesn't even fucking know it."

"You don't know anything. You don't know what it was like for me."

"Bad enough you almost killed your brother. Oh, sorry, not your brother. I guess that makes it okay."

"Fuck you."

"No, fuck you. First-born Scafoni son. What a joke, you're not even that. And yet, you get everything. Every fucking thing you want, while the rest of us pay for it."

"How do you pay, Gregory?"

He just looks at me for a long time and I think I

see how he pays. I see what Helena sees. What she keeps trying to tell me. That aloneness.

Maybe it's that that draws her to him.

"Fuck. What the fuck is happening?" I ask no one.

I sit on the canoe, run a hand through my hair.

"I fucked up, Greg. I have no excuse. I'm not making one. I fucked up. When I think about what happened, what I wanted to do—what I did do—to Ethan, I'm sick. I'm disgusted with myself."

"Yeah, well, that's not really good enough, is it? Not when you look at Ethan."

I look at the ground. He's right. "And I'm fucking up now. With her. With you."

"I just don't get it. God or karma or something should deal with you. Should make you pay. But here you are, king of the world. You get everything, and on top of it, she fucking loves *you*. You!"

I look up just in time to see him blink away, shake his head.

"After everything, she loves you. A real piece of work that one. Fucking masochist through and through. You two are perfect for each other."

I stand.

"What the fuck are you talking about?" I ask.

He turns back to me. "Like you don't fucking know."

"Helena."

"At least call her the fucking Willow Girl. At least fucking pretend that's all she is to you for my sake."

"She's been hurt. What Lucinda did—"

"Fuck what Lucinda did. Just fuck it. She's the fucking Willow Girl. It's what's supposed to happen. We're not supposed to fucking fall in love with her. You take her and you break her. It's the rule. And it will be when it's my turn."

"Greg." But all I hear in my head is: *"We're not supposed to fucking fall in love with her."*

Helena's wrong. He's not lonely.

He's in love.

Or at least he thinks he is.

"No. Fuck you, Sebastian. Just fuck you and fuck her and fuck it all. You let me have pieces of her while you watched. You let me touch her, but you want her eyes on you when I do. You punish her when she looks at me. You punish her when she comes and it's not on your dick. You know what? She's right. It's not fucking fair."

"I fucking shared her with you."

"To keep me under control. You think I don't know that?"

I step toward him, and he to me. A repeat of the other night.

"Because you wanted her," I say.

"And maybe she wanted me? A little at least? Is that what burns you up?"

My hands fist.

"Can't stand hearing that, can you? Well, don't do me any more fucking favors, *brother*. You keep her. For now. It's the rule. But when my turn comes, if you haven't burned your mark into her skin—and don't fucking tell me the thought of it doesn't make your dick hard because it sure does mine—well, let's just say I'll keep to the rules too. I'll take her. And I'll fucking break her and you'll both wish you'd been the one to do it because when I'm done with her, there will be nothing left. Nothing."

19

HELENA

Gregory is gone when I get downstairs later that night. His place isn't set for dinner and one of the boats is missing. Sebastian looks like he's on his second bottle of whiskey, just sitting there watching the fire, refilling his glass.

I slip into the seat beside his. Gregory's seat.

"Where is he?"

He doesn't look away from the fire, just shrugs a shoulder.

"You fought?" I ask.

"Yeah."

"Over me?"

"Over a lot of things." He turns to me, gives me a smile that's the saddest smile I've ever seen. "And he was right."

"Right about what?"

"Everything. Ethan. You. Me." He shakes his head. "He must hate me. And I deserve his hate."

"No, you don't," I reach out, touch his hand.

It's like he doesn't even feel it.

"You're right, too, Helena. This whole thing, it destroys us as much as it destroys you."

"Sebastian—"

"The Willow Girl. Taking her. This insane covenant, it leads to our destruction as much as yours." He picks up the bottle of whiskey to pour himself some more, splashes the liquid on the table. "You know we stopped once."

"Maybe it's enough," I say, trying to take the bottle away. He's had too much already.

He pulls it back. "I'll say when it's enough."

"Sebastian—"

"Two generations didn't do it. That's when we started dying. That's when the first-born son started to die."

"What are you talking about?"

"Used to be four of us. The Willow Girl would serve four brothers over four years. But when they didn't take a girl, it was like we cursed our own line."

"You can't believe that."

He shrugs a shoulder. "It's recorded, actually. From the beginning. If the Scafoni sons fail to uphold their end of the bargain, they're punished. It's to keep it going. To never forget our duty."

"Sebastian, you know that makes no sense."

"Timothy and me being twins, it's the first time that's happened. Maybe, since we've been taking Willow Girls...maybe the curse is finished. Maybe we paid."

"Curse?" Doesn't he hear how ridiculous this sounds?

"Maybe my sons will survive."

I snort, shake my head. "To carry on this sick tradition?" I get up, walk away. "To destroy more lives?"

"You destroy us too, remember that." He puts his glass down on the table and rises. "Walk with me."

He doesn't give me a choice but takes my hand, weaves his fingers through it and we walk.

"Where are we going?" I ask, pulling back when he doesn't answer, when I realize where he's taking me. "Sebastian?"

"Mausoleum."

I stop. "Why?"

"You know why."

I try to pull free. "No. I don't want to go there."

"You've been there already. Even though I told you that you weren't allowed."

I don't answer, he's not expecting me to.

"I want to show you something," he says.

"I don't like it there, Sebastian."

"Nothing's going to happen to you, Helena."

The way he's looking at me, I don't know if it's

the liquor or what, but it's intense and a little scary, actually.

"Let's go tomorrow. During the day."

He almost chuckles at that. "They're ghosts, Helena. They can't touch you."

We walk on, because it's no point arguing with him. If he wants me to be there, I'm going to be there. He'll carry me kicking and screaming if he has to.

I see the glow of the red light as we near the clearing and I swear the angel's visible eye shines in the moonlight.

We walk past the entrance to the main room, though, like I know we will. He walks me around the side of the building and takes out his phone, shines it on the gate of the entrance around the back.

The lock is lying on the ground. I wonder if it had fallen off after I'd run away from here. If he thinks it was me, he doesn't say anything but pulls the chain out and opens both gates wide. He shines his light inside.

"What's down there?"

"What you read about in your Aunt Helena's journal."

He takes my hand, the one with the ring. "This doesn't belong to you."

I feel that strange sensation again, that burning where Cain Scafoni's bone circles my finger.

"It belongs in the ground," he says. "Here."

I pull my hand away. "Not yet."

Not yet. But later, when this is over. When this legacy is no longer that, when it's finished once and for all. When I end it.

Because I'll be the last Willow Girl.

I know it.

Even if it costs me my life, I know I'll be the last.

A shudder runs through me.

"Not yet," I repeat quietly.

Sebastian studies me and he nods, and I wonder if he's thinking the same thing. That we'll bury it when this is over. Really over.

"Sebastian," I ask, stopping him when he takes a step toward the stairs that lead underground and into that inky black.

He turns to me.

"Do you want it to be over?" I ask.

His forehead is creased, it has been all night. Like he's deep in thought and maybe mourning.

He nods once, then turns and shines the flashlight of the phone down into the mouth of this dark cavern before disappearing into it.

"Come," he calls.

I take a tentative step, my heart racing, wondering how I'd done it earlier, how I'd gone down there. I'm terrified of it, of the energy coming from it, like that dank smell of a rotting mouth.

"Helena." He comes back up and I can see a

corner of his face and his outstretched hand. "Come."

I reach for his hand and shudder, but take a step forward, then another and soon we're walking down into this forsaken place, and with each step, the temperature drops, until it feels like a cold, damp winter day.

I count the steps, thirteen of them.

Unlucky.

Something scurries across the floor and I scream and if it weren't for Sebastian holding me, I'd turn and run back up those stairs and out of that condemned place. Out into the night and to the sanctuary of the house.

"It's a rat. Just a rat."

"Have you been down here before?"

"Yes," he says, and shines the flashlight over the room. It's bigger than the one upstairs and I see along the walls more Scafoni ancestors. We walk toward one and on one of the few where I can still read the inscription, I see it dates back to the 1700s.

"We'll need to add a floor," he says, and I am not sure if he's joking.

"This is creepy. Can we go?"

"Not yet."

He doesn't let go of my hand and I'm grateful for that as he leads me around the room and I see along the walls where torches must have been placed at one point to provide light.

But it's not that that has my attention. It's the large stone slab at the far end, the one that stands before the altar as if waiting for its sacrifice.

We go to it and Sebastian releases me to wipe off cobwebs, but they're too thick and an inch of dust or dirt sits on top of every flat surface.

"There should be a sanctuary light here too. Like upstairs."

He searches with the flashlight on the ground while I try not to hear the sound of rats or other animals and hug my arms to myself.

"Are we done?" I ask.

"Come here," he says.

I go to him and he holds the phone out to me. "Hold it."

He crouches down and reaches to pull at what looks to be a heavy chest almost buried by dust.

"What is it?" I ask.

His muscles work as he frees it, then stands back to look at it.

"Your aunt, what she wrote about the marking ceremony." He reaches down and opens it. "I didn't realize the middle brother had branded her his."

"Branded?"

He nods. Hauls the heavy lid open. Inside are various objects, none of which I can make out or give a name too. Sebastian, though, he crouches down again and he's looking through it, rummaging for something.

"She was blamed for Cain's murder, but it was his brothers, according to her journal at least. Which makes sense. I can't imagine she'd have been strong enough to smother him."

He finds what he's looking for. Four somethings.

He straightens, sets them on the altar.

"What are they?" I ask, but I think I know.

He picks up the first iron. It's about a foot long. The handle is woven metal with a few inches of worn wood and it has three prongs that end in a flat almost circular shape but not quite. There are markings, four compartments almost.

He puts that first one down and picks up the second, discards that as well and when he gets to the third, takes that one.

"This one's mine." He holds it up for me to see.

"What is it?"

"The coat of arms you saw on the front door, did you notice there were three smaller ones along the base of the door?"

I shake my head. I hadn't looked that closely.

"See this here," he points to a mark of some sort with a crescent shape. It means nothing to me. "Second-born. It's mine. This one here," he says, pointing to another one. "This is Ethan's, and this is Gregory's. Depending on your place in the pecking order, you have a symbol." He picks up the last one. "This would have been Timothy's."

"Why are you showing me these? What are they used for?"

"They're passed down from generation to generation. Each brother has his. This is what Gregory said to me in Gallo's office. What you were asking about."

"I don't understand."

"You do. But I'll explain anyway. See, there is a way out. Your aunt took it. If one of the brothers wants to keep the girl, she has to agree to be marked as his."

This is insane. Stuff from the dark ages.

I endured the marking ceremony.

"It has to be her choice. It can't be forced. This would have been the brand my great-uncle would have burned into your Aunt Helena's skin to claim her. See, another way the Willows destroy us. Destroy our family."

"You kidnap us. We have no choice."

"I'll give you a choice, Helena."

"What are you saying?"

"Do you want him?"

"What?"

"Do you want him? My brother?"

"Are we back to this?"

"Because he will claim you. He told me as much. It's why I was sharing you, hoping it wouldn't come to that. Hoping he'd be happy enough to leave it be. Leave you be."

"What?"

"He'll take you from me when the time comes."

"I won't go."

"It won't be your choice. Not then. Not anymore. That's why I'm giving it to you now."

"He can't make me."

He laughs outright. "Really? Look around you. Where are you? We can make you do anything we want."

I don't have an answer.

"He'll take you and he'll break you. He swore it."

"He wouldn't...hurt me."

"You don't know him."

"That's what he says about you."

"Unless I mark you as mine."

I hear him. And even though I understood what this was about, it's different to hear him say it. To hear it out loud.

"You'll brand me?"

Sebastian nods.

"With that?"

He doesn't nod or answer, but I see it in his eyes.

I shake my head and back away and run up the stairs, tripping, catching myself on the filthy, damp stone. Once I'm outside, I run to the house. I think about what I saw on my Aunt Helena's neck during my dream. It was the edge of the brand. It explains why, no matter how warm it got, she'd wear high turtlenecks.

Why she always kept her neck covered.

She hadn't wanted to show her shame.

That she'd loved a Scafoni monster.

Loved him enough to let him burn his mark into her skin.

20

SEBASTIAN

When we were little, my brothers and I would go down to that older part of the mausoleum to play chicken. We scared the shit out of each other. Gregory in particular was good at it. Even though Ethan was older than him, Greg could still get him.

Lucinda caught us once. I was ten or eleven and I still remember it clear as day. Hell, that's one memory I wish I could forget.

The mausoleum was off limits for us. One of the few things that was. We never let that get in the way though. It was one of the best places to play, especially after dark.

She only found us because we'd been stupid enough to light one of the torches we'd found for light. It was the first time we got a proper look at the place and I remember the stink of the rat that was decomposing in the corner. We'd found some sticks and were poking at various parts of it.

I'll never forget the sound of her heels as she descended the stairs—slow and calculated steps, our fear mounting with each one.

That was part of the thing with her. She liked scaring the shit out of us. She'd even do it to Ethan and Gregory from the time they could walk.

She blamed me, of course. That wasn't anything new. I thought she'd just cane me, like she always did. It hurt like fucking hell, but I knew the risks by then and I manned up when it came time to take my punishment.

I wouldn't let her cow me. Wouldn't let her think she had the upper hand, not even when she lay stroke after stroke down. I never cried. Never made a sound. And it probably only made things worse on me.

But that night, Lucinda got creative.

She led my brothers up the stairs but when it came time for me to walk through the gate, she stopped and turned to me. With only a grin instead of words, she closed the gate slowly and wove that chain through, delighting in drawing it out, relishing the fear on my face.

"Sleep with the dead tonight, Sebastian. See how they like it when you disturb them."

I'll never forget her words. I still shudder at the memory and I understand Helena sleeping with the lights on. I did for a long time after that because that torch we'd lit, it lasted about an hour and I'd still had the long, black night ahead of me.

I'd been so scared, that at one point, I'd pissed myself.

I'm not scared anymore though, or I'm too drunk to care. I take my time to collect the irons. They're heavier than you'd think. I make my way in the dark and head up the stairs. Thirteen. I've memorized them. I also know that the smell of earth will cling to my clothes and fill my nostrils for hours or days.

I walk back to the house, drop the irons on the table on the patio and sit down. I don't take my eyes off them as I drink whiskey straight from the bottle.

I want tonight to be over.

Today to never have happened.

I want to erase it.

When I finally I get up, I knock my knee into the leg of the table. Muttering a curse, I go inside, climb up the stairs to Helena's room.

"Helena." I hear myself, hear how I sound.

She either doesn't hear me or pretends not to and I'm going to bank on the latter. I hear the shower going in her bathroom.

She must want the stench of the mausoleum off. I do too.

I strip off my clothes and drop them on the floor. Without knocking, I go into the bathroom.

She's surprised to see me, which I guess

surprises me because by now, she's got to know how I operate.

I push the shower door open and step inside, take the loofah out of her hands and toss it aside.

"Why did you run?"

"I don't like that place."

"Yeah, well, it's not my favorite either." I look at her, naked, her skin glistening as water glides over it. I cup her breast, weigh it. I can't get enough of her.

"You want to do that to me?" she asks.

I look up at her face and admittedly, I'm way past anything resembling even remotely sober. My reactions are slow, to say the least.

I press her back to the wall and slide my hand down to cup her pussy.

"Do I want to brand my mark on you?"

I'm hard. My brother was right. The thought of branding her makes my dick hard.

Reaching behind her, I switch off the water and look at her as I rub her pussy. I dip my head down to take a nipple into my mouth.

"Do you?" she asks again when I don't answer right away.

"I can't get enough of you, Helena," I say, kissing her. "I want all of you. I have never wanted anything or anyone as badly as I want you and I just...I can't seem to get fucking close enough."

She swallows, slides her hands over my arms, to my shoulders.

"Do you want to hurt me like that?"

"Hurting you gets me off. But it also gets you off." I pinch her clit and she winces, but licks her lips, arches her back. "Point."

I lift her in my arms to carry her into the bedroom. I lay her on the bed, climb on top of her.

"You said the Willows have a sickness, well, I think we Scafonis are just as sick."

I slide into her pussy, watching her as I do. I like watching her face like this, seeing her take me when she's stretched too tight.

I kiss her.

"What's your sickness?" she asks.

"I want you. I can't stop thinking about you." I grip her hair, tug her head back. "You're under my fucking skin and I'm destroying my family for you."

She watches me, eyes huge, locked on mine like she's holding her breath.

"Who ever thought it'd just be the Willows who suffer?" I shake my head, think about the ridiculousness of it all. Wonder if it's always been this way between the Willow Girl and her Scafoni master. "I'm human. And I want you. I want you to want me. Fuck. Maybe I even love you in some sick, twisted way."

Love.

I grip her hair and force her head back. I don't want her to miss this next part.

"You should run like hell, Helena, because when

I think about you, your back bared, ready to take my brand, it makes my dick hard."

She shoves against me, obviously shocked by what I've just said. I grip her wrists, hold them both in one of my hands and thrust in hard.

"I told you, it's sick. Twisted."

"Sebastian, you're drunk."

I nod, thrust once more before sliding out, getting off the bed, stumbling backward.

I don't want to fuck anymore. This is more than that. This night. This day. All of this.

"My brother's right. Karma or God or something should deal me my punishment. God knows I deserve it for the things I've done."

She sits up, takes a nightshirt from under her pillow and slips it over her head.

I look down at the pile of clothes on the floor. "That smell will never come out. We'll have to burn them," I say, walking to the door that connects our rooms. It takes two tries to get my hand on the doorknob, to push it open.

"Sebastian." Helena's beside me.

"Go back to your own bed, Helena."

"No."

I don't know if it's the alcohol or the day, but I can barely stand and flop down on the bed.

"Go to bed. I'm telling you. Leave me alone," I say.

She climbs in beside me, wraps her arms around me. "No."

I manage to roll onto my side to face her. "I'm so fucking tired, you know that?"

"I know."

I touch her face with just my fingertips. "I'm going to hurt you. You should go back to your room. Away from me."

We just look at each other for a long time and she reaches up to touch my cheek.

"You won't hurt me," she says, burrowing into my chest. "And I can't sleep without you."

———

My head is throbbing when I wake up. Helena's gone and the clock on the nightstand tells me it's afternoon.

It takes me a minute to sit up.

I walk into the bathroom, swallow two ibuprofen, then decide on two more. I switch on the shower and step under the flow. I remember what happened last night, what I said, and I don't know if it's a blessing or a curse that I never forget a damn thing. Not one.

When I'm finished, I pull on a pair of jeans and head downstairs bare chested and barefoot. I see Helena before she sees me. She's got a fire going and is holding one of the branding irons in it.

Fuck.

I'd left them out. Why in hell did I even carry them out of that tomb? I should bury them.

"What are you doing?" I ask.

She startles, turns. Her eyes scan me, hovering over my shoulders and stomach before returning to mine.

"How do you feel?" she asks with a smug little grin.

"Fucking rude to answer a question with a question," I mumble and walk into the kitchen to get a cup of coffee since they'd already cleared breakfast. I drink a big swallow and arrange for bacon and eggs before returning to the patio to wait for the food. I sit in my place at the table.

"Why do you have that?"

"It was here. This one's yours, right?" she asks, pulling it from the fire, pointing to the crescent. It's so hot, it's glowing orange.

"God damn it, Helena," I say getting to my feet, taking it from her. I walk it out to the pool and stick the brand in the water and listen to it hiss and smoke.

Helena comes up behind me. "That's what you want to do to me?"

I look at her.

"Will it end things? End the Willow Girl legacy?"

"No. Even if it saves you, this tradition will continue."

She turns away, shakes her head. "But it still makes your dick hard to think about burning this into my skin."

I drop the still steaming iron on the ground by the pool. "I was fucked up last night. Said some stupid shit."

"You remember?"

"Yeah."

"I don't know. I think it was the truth, Sebastian."

"I have a headache, Helena. Leave me in peace."

Someone clears their throat and sets my dish down.

Helena sinks into my brother's empty chair. I didn't think I'd actually miss him.

I sit in mine and pick up my fork.

"Why did you drink so much?"

"Because yesterday was a shitty day all around."

"Because of your brother?"

"It's not his fault. It's mine. It's this whole situation."

"Why did you take me there? Why did you show me those irons?"

"I don't fucking know. I wouldn't do that to you, Helena. Even if you wanted it."

"Even if it means giving me to your brother?"

My jaw tightens.

"If I said yes—"

"No."

"But if I said—"

"I said fucking no. It's not up for discussion."

"Isn't this the point? Ultimately, doesn't it come down to this?"

I rub my eyes, my face.

"Fine. Answer me another question and I'll leave you alone," she says.

I nod.

"Why did you test me? With the phone call?"

I sigh deeply. "It wasn't so much testing you, Helena. I could see things between you and my brother and I didn't like it. That's all."

"You knew I'd get angry at him that he didn't tell me that you knew."

I nod.

"What about him? Did you want him angry with you too?"

"I think he loves you," I say rather than answering her question.

She's surprised, I can see that.

"That's not possible," she says.

"Why not? Wouldn't it be more surprising if he didn't? I mean, you're the one who tells me all the time that he's lonely."

"Not lonely. Alone."

"Doesn't matter. This thing, this whole situation, him like he is, with us all the time, me sharing you with him, he'd have to be a robot not to fall in love with you or at least think himself in love with you."

"No. You're wrong. He doesn't love me. This is a

pissing contest. He wants me because you have me. He wants his own Willow Girl."

"Do I have you?" I ask, my mind suddenly clear as day.

She studies me, doesn't answer.

"Because I want you, Helena. What I said last night. I remember that too. And I still think you should run like hell from me. From any of us. Because when this is over," I start, shaking my head as I think, pushing my plate away before I return my gaze to hers. "When this is over, I'll still want you. I love you. And I'm warning you to run like fucking hell because you're right. This isn't going to end well for you. For me. For any of us."

She reaches out to put her small hand over mine.

"You have me, Sebastian. And like last night, you can't make me go anywhere. I need you. I love you."

Her eyes fill up and I watch her.

"This is what happens. This is what no one counts on. I think my Aunt Helena loved your uncle. I think my Aunt Libby, she may have loved your father. As fucked up as it is, this is the saddest part of all of this."

21

SEBASTIAN

The next week is about the most peaceful week I have ever spent on that island. Even as a child, it's always been bittersweet. Too much tragedy, too much grief and hate and death. But this week, it feels different.

Fall is coming, and the cool air feels good after the heat of the last weeks. The change will be good. We need the change, Helena and me.

But I feel the loss of my brother more acutely than I thought I would. I think she does too, but neither of us talk about it. Gregory hasn't called and every message I've left has gone unanswered.

I think about Ethan too. For years, I've let what happened sit in the back of my mind, his presence a constant reminder of what I'd done, and, in a way, that was punishment enough. But I'm not thinking of my own punishment now. I owe Ethan. I owe him a better life than one spent under Lucinda's thumb.

"Can I try my sister again?" Helena asks as I swallow the last of my coffee.

I nod, hand over my phone.

She's been trying Amy for the last week but, like my calls to Gregory, they go directly to voicemail. A call home confirmed that Amy had done what she threatened to do. She left. No one knows where she is, and her phone's been offline.

After a few moments, Helena disconnects the call, disappointed. She doesn't leave a message this time. She sets the phone back on the table.

"She probably doesn't want your parents tracking her. I'm sure she's fine." I don't know that though. "Let's get out of here for a while. Take a trip. It'll be good to have a change. Be around people."

"Wow. I never thought you'd say that last part," she says.

"Where do you want to go?"

Before she has a chance to answer, my phone vibrates on the table between us. We both look at the display.

It's Joseph Gallo. I pick up.

"Joseph."

"I have news," he says without a greeting. Ever since that night at his office, he's been hard at work trying to prove his loyalty to me and I think maybe I judged him too harshly.

"Lucinda?"

"Yes. I had a call from her. Seems she's in need of funds."

I smile. "I figured that was the way to smoke her out."

I froze hers and Ethan's accounts when they disappeared. Only then did I realize she's been stealing from him. Skimming money out of his account and putting it into hers. Stealing from her own son.

"You can always count on Lucinda to be Lucinda. Where is she?"

"Outskirts of Philadelphia."

"What's she doing out there?"

But I remember as I ask the question.

Her family had an estate there that was condemned years ago, while my mother was still alive. I have some vague memories of conversations about it and my father telling Lucinda to let it go, that he wasn't putting money into that dilapidated house.

"From a look through her bank statements, she's been rebuilding the Ayer house for years, Sebastian."

Ayer is her maiden name.

"How the fuck did we not know this? To rebuild a house of that scale requires significant capital."

"She was smart in how she did it, small enough increments you wouldn't notice the funds moved out of Ethan's account, especially if you have no cause to expect that she'd steal from her own son."

"I should have caught it," I say. I should have paid closer attention to the details.

"What's done is done. And the good news is even if you have a beautiful home, you need money to live and she's out of it. I told her I'd transfer funds as soon as possible so she'll sit tight. What do you want me to do?"

"Ethan's with her?"

"Yes."

"Okay. Good. I want you to do nothing. I'm heading out there now. Should be there within twelve hours."

"All right."

"Any word on Gregory?"

"Nothing yet."

"What about Amelia Willow?" I look up to find Helena's eyes on me.

"No. We'll keep looking. She'll turn up."

"Thank you, Joseph. You've been a good friend."

"Good luck."

"I've never relied on luck." I stand up and tuck the phone into my pocket. "Pack a bag. We're going to Philadelphia."

"Philadelphia?"

I walk her inside. "Not the destination I had in mind either."

With the private jet, we arrive in Philadelphia in the early evening. By the time we drive to the house which is about forty minutes outside the city, it's almost half past seven. The house is a huge, old, stone estate, a mansion boasting fifteen bedrooms and acres of land. I've only ever seen it in photographs and what I'm seeing now is vastly different from what was in those photos.

I'm surprised to find the gates open and the house lit up, cars that would make any collector envious lining the drive.

"I guess we're lucky she's throwing a party. I don't imagine she'd have let us through the gate."

"The house is huge," Helena says. She's sitting beside me as I park our car and kill the engine. She turns to me. "What's the plan?"

"We're crashing a party," I say, opening my door and stepping to her side to help her out.

It's a crisp fall night and Helena hugs her jacket to herself. I'm in jeans and a T-shirt. It's what I'd had on earlier that day.

I take Helena's hand and we walk toward the grand entrance of the house with its wide staircase leading to two oversized wooden doors. A man stands ready to open them, only momentarily eyeing our attire.

It's a fancy party. Just what I'd expect of Lucinda.

Lucinda is easy to spot. I see her before she sees me. She's standing on the bottom step of the grand staircase talking to a group of men and women. She's smiling and from the way she uses her arms, I think she's showing off the house.

I smile wide, squeeze Helena's hand, and stalk toward her.

The crowd disperses. I only see them in my periphery because my eyes are locked on Lucinda, dressed in black from head to toe, her body too skinny, gaunt rather than slender, lending an almost witchlike quality to her. I don't think the severe dark hair helps. Her natural is a mousy brown I remember from before.

We're almost to them before she notices us. I'm actually shocked how long it takes her. But the moment she registers our presence, her expression shifts to one of disbelief, then something close to horror.

"Lucinda," I say, coming to a stop a few feet from her. "If I'd known you were throwing a party, we'd have dressed for it."

It takes her a full minute to regain her composure. Long enough that the couples around her are looking questioningly at each other.

"Excuse me," Lucinda says, stepping through them and coming toward us. "My stepson is here. With his little *girlfriend*."

She stops a few inches from me, her eyes steady

on mine but then turns to Helena and touches her cheek to Helena's in greeting.

I see her lips move and feel Helena tense, but I don't hear what she says.

"Sebastian!" It's Ethan. He comes around the corner looking dashing in a tuxedo, smiling wide, holding a martini in one hand.

If you didn't know him, if you didn't hear him talk or see him interact, you'd think he was like us. Normal.

"Ethan," I say, feeling something different than my usual irritation.

I wonder how much of that annoyance was Lucinda's influence all these years. She was always with him wherever he went. I don't think that was out of motherly love either. But maybe I'm being judgmental.

"It's good to see you, brother," I say.

He reaches out to hug me, but stops, something like panic crossing his features when he sees Helena beside me.

He shifts his gaze from hers to mine.

"It's okay, Ethan." I look at him. "I know."

"You're not mad?"

"Not at you."

I turn back to Lucinda. "We need to talk. Now."

22

HELENA

The house is spectacular. It makes the one on the island seem almost provincial.

But I'd happily fly back to the island than be here in Lucinda's house. Even seeing Ethan, even though I know he isn't responsible for what he did, it's hard not to cringe away.

Lucinda, Sebastian and I gather in the library which spans the first and second floors. We're on the upper level.

There are enough people here that I don't think anyone notices that the hostess is missing.

It's a magnificent library, but I can tell it's unused, unloved. The scale and new-ness of it may make ours at the Willow house appear almost dusty, but I still prefer it to this one.

The seating looks brand new, too new to be comfortable, and it isn't. It's leather and old fashioned and masculine. I get the feeling all of this is here for show.

"I see you found your Willow Girl. All healed up, are you?" Lucinda asks me.

Sebastian doesn't waste any time after turning a circle around the place. He flashes a smile, one I know, one that sends a chill along my spine.

He takes Lucinda by the arms. Gives her a shake.

"Know that the only reason you're not dead is Ethan."

"How dare you threaten me? In my own house."

"Your house? I think Ethan's paid for the remodeling." He releases her, takes a seat on one of the chairs. "I'm glad to see you used high end materials, at least. I'll be taking it over."

"Like hell you will."

"You stole from your own son."

She does that thing where her left eye twitches, but she sits down and, oddly, lights up a cigarette she takes from a box on the side table. I've never seen her smoke or smelled it on her. I didn't know she did.

"You shouldn't smoke in the house. It's not good for the paint," Sebastian says.

"What do you want?" Lucinda asks. "You here to punish me? For what I did to her or what I did to you?"

"No, punishments are finished. You're finished."

"What do you want then?"

"I want you to disappear. I want you gone, out of Ethan's life, out for good."

She snorts. "So, when you out him he's left with nothing? I don't know how he can be a threat to you after what you did. You took care of that, didn't you?"

Sebastian's eyes narrow, but he takes it, even though it takes him a moment to reply.

"I'm not outing him. This is just a variation of the deal I offered you before. Except this time, you're going to accept it and you're going to do exactly as I say."

"Or what?"

"Or I *will* kill you, Ethan or not."

Lucinda looks at me, then back at Sebastian like she can't believe what she's hearing. I see how her hand trembles as she brings that cigarette to her mouth and draws in breath.

"Ethan will never be the wiser as far as his parentage. I, quite frankly, don't care who his father is. I'll be sure he's cared for *properly*. I'll be sure he has his rightful place as a Scafoni son."

"What does that mean?" she asks, a sideways glance at me.

"This has nothing to do with the Willow Girl. That's still off the table and, quite frankly, none of your concern."

"What do I get?"

"Money. The only thing you want. You'll have a

monthly allowance. A generous one. But you will never have contact with my brother again."

She taps ash into an ashtray, then smudges out the half-smoked cigarette altogether.

"You have no options, Lucinda. You're not welcome back on the island or in any Scafoni home. I'm making you this offer exactly once. You decide here and now. You take it, you say your goodbyes to Ethan, tell him whatever you want to tell him, and by tomorrow, you're gone. You don't take it, well, you're still gone."

His threat makes me shudder. I wonder if he's capable of that. Wonder how far he's willing to go.

"Ethan will take care of me."

"His accounts are managed by me now. He's not fit, as you know, and you've been taking advantage."

"He's my son, Sebastian."

"So is Gregory. I don't hear you crying over him."

She studies Sebastian, her watery eyes looking, for the first time since I've known her, afraid.

Sebastian stands.

"Helena," he says, holding out his hand to me.

I take it, get to my feet, but stop a few steps later.

"Why did you do it?" I can't help but ask. "Why kidnap me and leave me in that room like that? What do you get out of hurting me?"

Lucinda drags her gaze to mine.

"I've seen the destruction the Willow Girls leave behind. You think I like living it twice?" She rises slowly, never taking her eyes from me. "I hate you, all of you," she pauses. "I. Hate. You."

"Come on," Sebastian says to me, dragging me toward the door. "Let's go. You're not going to get anything of value out of her."

I shudder when we leave the library. It's literally like I'm shedding a cold, dead skin.

"You okay?" he asks.

"She's so full of hate. I've never known anyone like that." I lean against the banister, not realizing I was holding my breath. Downstairs a pianist plays classical music and guests mingle and drink champagne and eat canapés, blissfully unaware.

"Forget Lucinda," he says.

"A little underdressed, aren't you?"

I jump when I turn to find Gregory standing against the wall. I wonder how long he's been there. I wonder if he was listening at the library door.

He holds up his glass as if in greeting, then drinks.

Sebastian takes a step toward him. "What the hell are you doing here?"

"Visiting mommy dearest," he answers Sebastian but his eyes rest on me.

"Did you know she was here all along?"

He turns to Sebastian. "No. Just found out." I can't tell if he's lying or not. "How's our Willow Girl? I hope you're taking good care of her."

I can almost hear Sebastian seethe when

Gregory drags his gaze over me slowly, purposefully before stepping toward me.

"Find the irons?" he asks, his breath a whisper that makes me shudder and I wonder if that is what he's doing? Looking for a mark?

"I want to go," I say to Sebastian. "I don't want to be here."

"We're staying, Helena," Sebastian answers, eyes on Gregory. "We'll be here until I clear the house of vermin."

"Ouch," Gregory says. "Does that mean only retarded brothers are allowed to stay?"

An instant later, Sebastian and Gregory are nose to nose and I grab Sebastian's arm to try to pull him off.

"Stop it. Stop fighting!"

"This one's not over you, Willow Girl. Mind your own fucking business," Gregory says.

Sebastian takes hold of the collar of Gregory's dress shirt and drags him to the banister, pushing him backward over it. His back is bent at what must be a painful angle.

Gregory just grins at him, as if daring him to do more. To hurt him. To throw him over.

"Stop, Sebastian. You're going to hurt him. You're going to really hurt him!"

It takes him a long minute, but I watch as Sebastian takes in the people downstairs, looks at his brother, at how he's holding him.

It's another few moments before he pulls him up, releases him and steps backward.

"Are you okay?" I ask Gregory.

He straightens the sleeves of his jacket, eyes on Sebastian, who turns his back.

"Like you care, Helena," Gregory says. He shifts his gaze to me, finishes his drink which he somehow managed not to spill. "Like you give a fuck."

Again, I find myself exhaling as I watch him disappear down the stairs and out the front door, depositing his empty glass on a passing waiter's tray.

"Christ," Sebastian says.

"Please, let's go. Let's get out of here."

"I can't Helena. I have to make sure Lucinda does as she's told." He calls over a woman dressed in a uniform who comes out of one of the far rooms. "What's your name?" he asks her.

"Marion, sir."

"Marion. We need a room. Helena needs to lie down."

She looks at me with concern.

"Of course. This way, Miss."

"I don't need to lie down," I tell Sebastian.

"Go with her." His gaze is down the stairs. "I need to take care of some things. I'll be back as soon as possible."

"Don't go after him, Sebastian."

He turns to me, cups my face with his big hands.

"You'll be safe. No one's going to hurt you anymore. Go get some rest."

I don't have a choice, but between the time difference, the flight, Lucinda and, mostly, Gregory, I'm exhausted and I follow Marion into one of the bedrooms.

23

HELENA

Sebastian isn't back when I wake up. It's quiet and a glance at the window tells me it's still night.

I get up, hug my arms to myself for the chill. The clock on the nightstand says it's a little after three in the morning. I go to the window, which overlooks the back garden of the house. Even in the darkness, I can see the property is expansive.

In the bathroom, I splash water on my face, wondering where Sebastian is. Wondering how I fell asleep like I did.

When I open the door, the house is quiet. It's almost like there's no one here at all.

I step into the hallway and walk toward the stairs, pausing at the library doors, remembering.

It's dark now, I don't see any light from beneath the door. I'm barefoot so I don't make any sound, but it doesn't matter. There's no one around, just a single lamp left on in the living room and a few glasses left behind as evidence of anyone having been here.

I creep down the stairs and go to the front door. It's not locked, and I open it and I'm relieved to find the car we came in still parked in the same spot as when we got here.

I exhale, but what did I think? That Sebastian would leave me here?

There's another lamp left on in the large dining room. Here, clean crystal tumblers and flutes and a variety of wine glasses stand ready to be put away in the morning. I assume the door leading off the dining room is the kitchen and there's a sliver of light beneath the door.

I know it can be any one of them. Ethan or Lucinda or Gregory, but I go to it anyway, and I push it open a little.

But this room, too, is empty.

There's a bottle of whiskey on the counter and two glasses on the table, each with the remnants of the amber liquid inside. The label is familiar. It's the brand Sebastian and Gregory drink.

Finding a clean glass, I pour two fingers for myself. I don't know why, it's not like I like it, but I take it and sit down in one of the chairs at the table and sip.

I don't know where Sebastian is. There hadn't been a lock on the door for me to lock it, but maybe he didn't know which room I was in. Or maybe he drank so much again that he's passed out in one of the other bedrooms.

The kitchen door opens then, and a gust of cold wind blows in.

My heart leaps to my throat when Gregory steps inside.

He appears just as shocked to see me as I am to see him, and it takes him a minute before he closes the door and seems to regain his composure, which he does faster than me.

"Where's your bodyguard?" he asks, barely casting a glance around as he goes to the sink and runs water over the butt of his cigarette before tossing it into the trash can.

"Why do you smoke?"

"Why not?"

He turns to face me, leans his back against the counter.

"Are you worried about my health?" he asks.

He eyes my whiskey, brings the bottle over to sit down across from me. He pours into one of the two glasses there and swallows it all before pouring another.

"You drink too much, too," I say.

"Judgmental much?"

"You and your brother both do."

Plastering a false smile on his face, he takes another healthy sip.

"Think you should be here? Alone with me?" he asks.

I study him and again, I see it, that broken boy behind the angry, hard façade.

"Why are *you* here, Gregory? At Lucinda's house?"

"I didn't exactly feel welcome on the island."

"Are you welcome here?"

He shrugs a shoulder.

I look down at the amber liquid, swish it around, then take a sip.

"Does it help?" I ask.

"Does what help?"

"If I drink enough, will it all go away? Will I forget?" I ask. I look at his strange eyes, so dark with those specks of bright turquoise.

"Just for a while," he says.

He swallows the contents of his glass and gestures for me to do the same.

I pick it up and do it, even though it burns like hell, and he pours me another.

"That's a good Willow Girl."

"Stop with that. Just stop."

"Why?"

"Because it's not you. You're not a jerk even though you go out of your way to act like one."

He snorts. "That's where you're wrong, Helena. I'm a jerk and an asshole, but no more so than my brother."

"Where is he?"

He shrugs a shoulder. "I'm not Sebastian's keeper."

We sit in silence for a long minute.

"You're wrong," I say.

He raises an eyebrow.

"You're neither of those things. I see you, Gregory. I see past the asshole image you like to put on. It's just a front and I see through it."

"Really?" He drinks.

I take another sip, even though I'm feeling the alcohol.

"Yeah, really. What you said when we were on that beach, I get you wanting it. Wanting that stupid kiss. What Sebastian does, I know it's not fair, not to you."

"Fair," he snorts. "Life's not fucking fair, Helena."

"It's not." I'm quiet, considering my words.

"You know if he finds you in here with me, he'll be pissed," Gregory says.

"You don't care about that," I say.

"Do you?"

"I think sometimes, it's easier for me because he makes me. With you. When he tells me to, it's easier."

I balance the glass on its edge on the table, focusing on it rather than looking at him.

"Even when he punishes me after."

When I finally look up, I find him watching me.

"What do you want, Helena?"

I drink from my glass. I don't answer.

"What are you doing here?" he continues. "With me?"

"I care about you, Gregory."

"Bullshit."

"It's not bullshit. I do."

His eyes search mine. "But you love him."

I nod.

He pushes his chair back, scraping the tiles.

I get up too, catch his arm when he turns to go. "Wait."

He looks down at my hand wrapped around his wrist, then turns his gaze up to mine.

"Wait for what?" he asks.

The way he looks at me, it's like he's looking for something. Like he's searching like you would a buoy when you're out too far at sea and don't have the strength to swim another minute. Another second.

"Wait for what, Helena?" he asks again, shifting his hands so they wrap around both of my wrists and walking me backward toward the wall.

"Gregory—"

"No." He steps closer so he's looming over me. "Answer me. Wait for what?"

My heart races.

"I don't know what," I finally say.

He exhales, brings his mouth to my ear and I feel

the scruff of his jaw on my cheek and hear his warm breath on my ear.

"If you were mine I wouldn't share you," he whispers, making the hair on the back of my neck stand on end. He kisses the side of my cheek and I squeeze my eyes closed.

"Gregory, stop."

When I try to free myself, he tightens his grip on my wrists. He draws back just far enough so I can see his eyes.

"Did he do it?" he asks, touching his forehead to mine.

I lick my dry lips. "Do what?"

He gives the smallest, one-sided grin and transfers my wrists into one of his hands at my back. With the other, he reaches under my hair, behind my neck, feeling there, looking for something.

I know what.

"The mark. Did he do it?"

"You want him to brand me?"

He shifts his hold so he cups the back of my head, then squeezes his fingers in my hair.

"You're hurting me, Gregory."

"You like being hurt, Helena."

"What do you want? What do you want with me? Do you want me because you feel something for me or do you want me because I'm his?"

He tugs my head backward just a little, just enough. "What do I want?"

I grit my teeth, feel my eyes harden as I try to nod.

He holds me so tightly that I can't move and brings his mouth to mine.

When his lips touch mine, I make a sound, sealing them until he tugs my head backward, forcing them to open.

"Stop."

He sucks my lower lip into his mouth and he's soft and I like the taste of him, that of whiskey and the hint of cigarette smoke and him, and I think about how beautiful he is when he comes. How his eyes glisten when he comes.

He lets out a small, satisfied moan, then takes my lower lip between his teeth and all the while, he's watching me. Watching as he bites, just a little, just enough to break skin, to draw a taste of blood before pulling back and looking at me. Grinning.

"I like kissing you, Helena. I like it very much."

"He'll kill you."

"This is what I wanted," he says, ignoring my comment. "It was *all* I wanted. But you couldn't give it to me."

"Gregory—"

"You couldn't give me this one thing."

"Please, don't."

"I don't ask much." He kisses me again and this time, I manage to turn my face away.

"I love him!"

Anger flits across his features and he releases me like I've just burned him. Like I've just scalded his skin.

"Then prove it," he says. He steps backward as he wipes the corner of his mouth. "Do it."

I feel my eyes widen.

He smiles, but it looks wrong.

"Let him brand you and I'll know you mean it and I'll let you go. Or don't, and I'll take everything from him. The Scafoni inheritance. You. Everything."

"I'll hate you."

"I don't care. I did. But I don't anymore."

"You can't do it."

"I can. With Ethan out of the way, it can all be mine."

The kitchen door swings open and we both turn to find Sebastian standing there.

It takes him exactly one millisecond to look at us like this before he pounces.

Gregory's ready for him.

I press my back into the wall as the brothers go after each other, two giants battling, glasses shattering, chairs toppling over as they fight ruthlessly.

I scream.

Watching them, it's terrifying.

They're going to kill each other.

"Stop!" I cry out, wanting to physically stop

them, afraid to go near them. They're too big and too strong.

"You always want what's not yours," Sebastian says, his voice steel.

"No. Not always. Just now."

"Fuck you, brother."

Sebastian's fist almost sends Gregory to the floor, but a moment later, it's Sebastian who's taking a blow from Gregory, toppling backward into the kitchen table.

"Stop it! You're going to kill each other!"

But it's like I'm not here at all. Neither of them are listening to me. So I pick up the bottle of whiskey and hurl it against the far wall.

I don't know if it's the shattering of crystal or my scream that finally makes them stop. Finally makes them look at me.

"I'll do it. He'll do it," I say, my voice higher, panicked. I'm looking from one to the other.

"Quiet, Helena. This is between me and my brother," Sebastian says.

The way Gregory looks at him as he wipes blood from his temple, I think Sebastian is right. That all of this, it's always been between them.

None of this has ever been about me.

"I'll do it," I say again, more quietly this time. I sag back against the counter.

"I said quiet, Helena." Sebastian's voice, too, is quieter.

"No. Don't quiet her," Gregory says.

He steps away, lets out a small, strange laugh. His gaze burns into mine.

Sebastian steps toward me, wraps an arm around my waist. I lean into him, my knees buckling at what I'm agreeing to.

Gregory's voice is level when he speaks again. "Let her prove herself. If you do this, I'll relinquish my claim. She'll be yours."

He's talking to Sebastian, but his unblinking eyes are locked on mine.

"You can't ask that—" Sebastian starts, then stops. "Ask something of *me*. Not her."

Gregory finally turns to him. "That's not how this works, and you know it. There are rules. There's no other way." He takes a long breath in. "That's the thing, isn't it? We're all locked in. And this contract ensures our hate."

He shakes his head, takes two steps away.

"I wonder if it's always been like this," he says. "If our hate has always devoured us from the inside. Hell, we don't need a Willow Girl to destroy us. We manage just fine on our own."

"Brother—"

"No. No more brother." Gregory walks to the door. I've never seen him like this. "You claim her. Put your mark on her. And it ends. It ends for her, at least."

"Until the next crop," I say, my voice breaking.

I'm tired.

I'm out of fight.

"Tell me," I start, looking at Gregory. "Will it be your sons to take the next Willow Girl? Will it be you who teaches them to hate us?"

At that, Gregory almost flinches.

"There are rules," he says, shifting his gaze momentarily, running a hand through his hair again, and for one single, fleeting moment, letting me glimpse that loneliness, that alone part of him that makes my heart hurt.

I don't try to hold back the tears that are building as I watch him. As he watches me. As I lean closer into Sebastian, into his strength. Because I need it right now. I need him. And he'll need his strength to hurt me because it's the only way.

The only way to save me.

To save us.

24

SEBASTIAN

Helena and I have been back on the island for one full week. After that episode in the kitchen, Gregory disappeared. He left Lucinda's house and I haven't seen him since. And I haven't tried to contact him.

Lucinda did as she was told. She talked to Ethan, told him she needed to take a trip, a vacation on her own. Told him she'd send him postcards.

Ethan was more okay with it than I thought he would be. Hell, maybe he was relieved she left.

When I talked to him about it, told him that he'd stay at the house in Philadelphia, that it was his, a part of his inheritance as a Scafoni, and that I'd be back to visit him, he seemed excited, even. I didn't want to leave him until I was sure, but with the medical staff and help I hired, I know he'll be looked after even if it's not a long-term solution for him.

For the entire time we've been back, I've been poring over the Willow Girl Covenant, trying to find some way out of this. There isn't one, though. I already know it. I've always known it.

I have to hurt her if I want to keep her.

Helena is sitting at the table cradling a whiskey. She's been drinking it nightly since we got back.

I look at her, and she's looking tired.

"You want me to ask cook to prepare something else for you?" She's so anxious that she hasn't been able to keep anything down.

"No, thanks. I'm not hungry."

"I'll call a doctor. See if he can do anything."

"What's a doctor going to do?" she snaps, then lowers her gaze, realizes. Her tone is softer when she next speaks. "We just have to finish this. It's just going to get harder the longer we wait."

"We're not doing it his way, Helena. We have a year. We'll find another way."

She shakes her head. "We have to. What choice do we have?" She drinks her whiskey. "And really, don't we deserve this, you and me? What we did to him..." She runs her fingers through her hair. Her forehead is creased with worry. "What we did to him," she repeats, looking at me, "I never intended to hurt him. I know you didn't either. But we did hurt him. Together, we did. Being with him...what we did...he's human, Sebastian. And we hurt him."

"You talk like you have feelings for him."

"I do. I care about him. I don't want him to hurt. But that's all that means."

I struggle to understand this. It's selfish, I know, but rivalry and jealousy, they're tearing me apart. They've torn my family apart.

And I know she's right.

We have to do this. For everyone's sake. This branding, this ceremonial marking, the pain she will suffer, it will seal my claim to her, which will free her. And it will free my brother and me.

But I'll never forgive him for demanding it.

And I'll never forgive myself for doing it.

The sound of a boat engine has us both turn toward the dock.

"Mother fucker."

I stand up as I watch Gregory dock his boat, killing the engine. He steps off and stops. From the distance, I can see he's looking at me.

Helena stands too, and we watch as my brother approaches.

"Go up to your room, Helena."

"No."

I feel my hand squeeze around her arm, tightening as Greg nears, as I see the smile widening on his face.

"I said go to your room."

"You'll kill each other," she says.

I turn to her. "That's one way to end this, isn't it?"

But Helena doesn't have a chance to reply because we're no longer alone.

"Hello, brother."

I drag my gaze to his. "Helena." I don't look at her. "Go upstairs. Now."

"She responds better if you call her Willow Girl. Teaches her her place," Gregory says.

She's right. I'm going to fucking kill him.

"Helena," I say one last time.

"I'll go." I release her, and my brother and I don't take our eyes off each other as she disappears into the house.

Gregory walks around me to pick up a glass, fills it with whiskey. He sits down in his chair at the table. I didn't bother lighting a fire tonight. I wasn't in the mood.

I sit down, drink the last of my whiskey.

He pours more for me.

"Do you care about her?" I ask.

His eyes narrow.

"Or do you just want to hurt her? Because if you make her go through this, she will hate you."

"She already hates me, brother."

"Yeah, that's the thing. She doesn't." I shake my head, pick up the glass, then set it down again. "You're a fucking sadist, you know that?"

"And you're a saint?"

"What will you get out of this?"

"You should be thanking me. I'm saving you from

yourself. You do this, and you get to keep it all, including the girl."

"I don't fucking want it. I don't want anything but her."

He stops at this, then shakes his head and drains his glass.

"Think of this as karma coming to collect. For the first time in your life, you have to pay. Well, she pays for you, I guess. Story of your life. But I wonder if you'll ever be able to get the sound of her screams out of your head when you put the branding iron to her skin."

"We're finished after this. You're not my brother."

"That's fine," he bites through gritted teeth. "You and me, Sebastian, we were finished the day you laid eyes on her. You threw everything away for her, even me. So that's fine." He shoves the chair back and gets to his feet. "Tomorrow night. We do this then. Then I'm gone. And neither of you will ever have to see me again."

25

HELENA

I haven't been able to keep food down for days.
I'm terrified. I'm so afraid of the pain.
Tonight's the night.

In under an hour, in fact.

I haven't left my bed all day. When Sebastian came up to see me, I sent him away.

I'm lying here reading my Aunt Helena's journal again for the hundredth time, trying to syphon strength from it, trying to muster the courage to get through this.

The sheath I wore on the night the Scafoni brothers came to the Willow house and Sebastian Scafoni made me the Willow Girl hangs from a hook on the door.

We're back at the beginning. We've come full circle.

I never thought this was where I'd be when he

took me. I hated him. And I wanted to keep hating him. Hating them. Yet, even now, even knowing Gregory is forcing this, I don't. I don't hate either of them.

My door opens, and Sebastian enters. His face is unreadable, as if made of stone. His jaw is tight. He's struggling against this.

"Is it time already?" I ask.

He gives a short nod.

"Don't do this, Helena," he finally says. "Don't make me do this to you."

I push the covers off and climb out of the bed. I'm naked but it hardly matters.

Walking past him, I pull that hated sheath off its hanger and slide it over my head. Ceremony. I have to wear this rotting thing again.

I look at the stain of pig's blood on the front. It was supposed to save me.

Maybe in a way, it did.

I look up at him, touch his face.

"I love you."

He takes my wrist but doesn't pull my hand away.

"I don't know how you can."

"Where will it be?" I begin to tremble.

He knows what I'm asking. He reaches behind my neck and a little to the side to touch a spot. "Here."

I nod.

"Take these," he says, holding out two pills.

"What are they?"

"They'll knock you out. You won't feel it, not when it's happening."

"How?"

"Sedative. Same stuff they gave you after Lucinda. You have to take them now and walk out with me. If you pass out at the post, Gregory will think you passed out from fear."

I nod, take the pills. Swallow them dry.

"What about when I wake up?"

"I have pain medication already. Strong stuff. You can take it until it heals. Until you don't feel any pain."

I nod again. What can I say that won't make him feel worse than he already does?

"I'm sorry, Helena. I'm so sorry."

It takes all I have to force the smallest smile. "Let's get this over with." I'm already feeling the pills.

Sebastian holds onto me as we descend the stairs. The scent of the fire outside makes my stomach heave and I think I'd throw up if I had eaten anything more than the two crackers I managed earlier. The patio doors are open, as usual, and I shudder at the cool air when we walk outside.

"You can change your mind," Sebastian says as we walk toward the post where a second fire is burning. Where, in the light of that second fire, Gregory stands waiting.

"No, I can't." My knees buckle once, and Sebastian catches me.

"Steady."

"I'm okay." I stop before we'll be in earshot of Gregory and turn to him. "Thank you."

"You have nothing to thank me for. Not a goddamn thing."

I put my hands on either side of his face and he has to hold me up because it's taking all I have not to fall down and I don't think it's the pills. It's fear.

"Please don't do this," he tries once more.

"I'm glad it'll be you to do it, not him."

"It's going to kill me."

I shake my head, kiss his mouth. Then kiss it again.

"I love you. I love you so much," I say.

He pulls me tight to him and for a moment, I'm not sure if he isn't going to carry me off the island, run away with me, but instead, he lifts me up and carries me to the post. My head bobs against his chest and my eyes are closing, so I have to struggle to keep them open.

Gregory comes into view a few minutes later. He's dressed in black from head to toe and I realize Sebastian is too.

Behind Greg, the fire sparks and hisses angrily, and I turn my head into Sebastian's chest when I see the branding iron inside it.

"Tell me to stop." He sounds tortured, like he's

the one about to be branded. "Tell me to fucking stop this."

I shake my head no, try to squirm out of his arms.

But he won't let me go, not even when we're at the post, where Gregory stands watching like that angel over the mausoleum. Dark and beautiful and constant and scary as fuck.

He doesn't say anything, nothing cocky or arrogant or anything at all. And his expression is somber, and he won't stop looking at me.

"It's okay," I say to Sebastian, whose eyes are burning into his brother, murdering him with just a look. "I can stand."

He looks down at me and I've never seen him like this. His eyes, like this. Full of anxiety and hate and pity and remorse and everything all at once.

Gregory moves, taking hold of one of my arms as Sebastian sets me down. He raises it over my head and I think if he let it go, it'd flop down to my side. I think if Sebastian lets me go and if I'm not bound, I will drop to the ground.

Sebastian raises my other arm and secures me and it takes all I have to straighten my legs, to stand on them.

I rest my forehead on the post. Even though it's cool, I'm sweating and I hear them talking behind me but I must be going in and out of consciousness because I can't follow what they say. I just hear them argue before I feel something wrap around my middle and I scream.

"Shh," It's Sebastian. "It's not it. Not yet."

He pushes the hair from my face to make me look at him and I'm having a hard time keeping my eyes open but I'm not sure why I'm struggling against the pills. I want to be knocked out cold when they do it. When he burns his mark into my skin.

I look down and watch him tie the belt around me and the post, hugging me to it.

"So you don't move. So we only do it once."

I don't understand but I don't care.

"Did you give her something?" I hear Gregory ask. "She's out of it."

"She's fucking terrified, you asshole. How with it would you be if it was you tied to the damn post?"

"Fuck you."

I hear the scuffle and I turn my head, rest my cheek against the post.

"I'm scared," I manage, my eyes closing again. The last image I see is Gregory's face, his eyes on me, the look inside them that tells me this isn't what he wants. Not how he wants it.

But then he steps behind me and picks up my hair and puts the length of it over my shoulder and I scream when I feel him rip the sheath in two, the sound jarring as he bares my back, prepares it for the iron.

And then his hands that can be so cruel, so

merciless, are warm and soft on my neck and he cups the back of my head and just before I pass out, he says something. I feel the whisper of his breath. Just a few words before I'm out, the pills doing their work, saving me from the heat of the fast approaching iron.

26

SEBASTIAN

Helena's passed out. The belt binding her to the post takes some of the pressure off her wrists, but her knees are bent and Gregory's holding her head against the post or it would flop to the side.

I look at my brother.

His eyes are dark, burning as intensely as the fire.

I didn't hear what he whispered to her. I wonder if she did or if she was already gone. But now he turns to me.

"You gave her something," he says again.

"Yeah, I did. She's fucking terrified. You need her awake so you can hear her scream? That's not anywhere in the rules."

He swallows. I see his throat work.

"You can still change your mind," I say. "Not for me, but for her."

He shakes his head once.

I pick up the iron, even the wooden handle feels hot, but I grip it, hold it tight. I want it to burn me. Burn me and not her.

Fuck.

Not her.

Gregory pushes the torn sheath from her shoulder, exposing most of her back, and I step closer.

There's a flash of electric light in the distance, and a moment later, thunder breaks the silence of the night.

It's going to rain.

It's going to pour.

I step closer, touch her skin, touch the smooth flesh I will scar.

She doesn't move at all, not even when I push my fingernail into her skin, testing. And I raise the branding iron and its bright orange glow sickens me.

Gregory shifts his grip on her and I think for a minute I'd love to shove it in his face. I'd love to burn it into him. Mark him with it. Destroy him.

And just when I think I will, just when I'm inches from her and him, he shoots out his arm and closes his hand over the hottest part of the iron and squeezes his fist and I hear his pain, hear it through his gritted teeth as the iron loudly sears the skin of his hand.

Time stops.

I don't do anything.

I can't.

It takes me a full minute to register what he's done.

What he's doing.

I drag my gaze from his hand to his face and I see his pain, I see the torment on his face and finally, I tug the brand away and he pulls his hand free and when he stumbles backward, he knocks the fire basket over scattering the fire, sending flaming wood toppling downhill.

For a moment, I think he's caught fire. But then he looks at me again and he looks at her again and I wonder if he'd planned this all along. If he'd never intended on letting me brand her. If this was his test for me. I wonder if he'd planned on saving her from it at the last second.

Like a pardon just before the ax falls.

I drop the iron to the ground.

"Brother."

But he doesn't answer. He's gripping his arm, smoke coming from the injured hand. I only see it for a second, only glimpse the damage for one second before he walks away. Walks back to the house.

I don't go after him.

I let him go.

And I watch him disappear before turning my

attention back to Helena and undoing the bonds at her wrists, supporting her as I unbuckle the belt—Gregory's belt—and lift her in my arms.

She's unconscious, the drug will keep her out for a while. I carry her back into the house and upstairs to my room and lay her on my bed. I tear that sheath from her and I think I want to burn it in that fire too. I want it gone. I want everything that has anything to do with the Willow Girls gone. Gone from my life. Gone from hers. Gone from my brother's.

And when I look at her lying naked in my bed, I lie down beside her, and I hold her, and I don't think I'll ever let her go again.

27
HELENA

I expect pain when I begin to wake. I anticipate it, even through the black fog of the drug. But what I feel when I open my eyes is nauseous.

I stumble out of bed and I'm naked, but I hardly pay attention as I run to the bathroom.

Sebastian is behind me in a heartbeat but when I get there, nothing happens. I haven't eaten anything in too long for there to be anything to throw up.

When the wave passes, I collapse onto the floor, my back to the wall.

Sebastian looks like a ghost. His face is white, his eyes ringed with shadows like he hasn't slept in weeks. He's still wearing the same clothes as last night and I can smell the smoke of the fire on him.

And I don't feel anything. No pain.

I reach back, touch the space where I should have been branded, but there's nothing there.

Sebastian leans back, puts his hand to his forehead.

I touch him. Pull his hand away.

He looks broken.

"What happened?"

He doesn't answer. I've never seen him like this.

"Where's Gregory?"

Oh God. Did he hurt him? Kill him? Because no matter what he believes, he won't survive injuring another brother. And not this one. It'll destroy him.

"Sebastian?"

"He's gone."

"Gone where?"

"He left. A few hours after."

"What happened?"

He's looking off in the distance, and he's got his hand covering his mouth, then his throat.

"He closed his hand over the brand."

"Oh, my God."

"Fuck. Helena, he..."

I go to him, wrap my arms around him, hug him to me.

"I gave him every chance to stop it, but he refused. And when I was holding the iron just inches from you, he reached out and grabbed it."

"He burnt himself on purpose?"

Sebastian nods. "He didn't have to. If he wanted it stopped, all he had to do was say the word."

"Jesus."

"What did I do?" He's got his face in his hands. "How in hell did we get to this place?"

I peel his hands away, cup mine on either cheek to make him look at me.

"You didn't do anything," I say. "He did this. He wanted it. He chose it. He did this. This isn't your fault."

He studies me, leans his head back against the wall.

"I didn't know him." He stands up, goes to the sink and runs the water, splashes some on his face, then turns off the taps and looks at his reflection. "Not at all," he says.

I get to my feet, go to him, put my hand on his shoulder.

But he shoves me away and in the next instant, smashes his fist into the mirror, shattering it, swearing, cursing God and his family and mine.

I jump backward, sharp pieces of the mirror falling almost in slow motion around my bare feet, the sound almost musical as slivers cut into my legs.

Sebastian's hand is bleeding when I go to him, stepping over shards like knives. I take his hand in both of mine, pull out the pieces.

I feel his other hand close around the back of my head, caress my hair.

"It's not your fault," I say to him as I clean his hand.

When I look up at him, he's watching me, and

his face, he just looks like a little boy. Like Gregory sometimes did.

Lost.

He cups the back of my head, pulls me to him, kisses me hard. It's not erotic, it's something wholly different and he doesn't stop as he lifts me up and carries me into the bedroom.

He pulls off his shirt as he climbs on the bed. The cuts from his hand leave smears of blood on my skin. He kisses me again, and this, what we're doing, it's not sensual or lustful or any of those things. It's need. Pure need.

Sebastian's full weight on me makes it hard to breathe. He shifts onto one elbow, still kissing me, still watching me as he reaches to undo his jeans and push my legs wider. I cling to him and I'm not ready when he pushes into me but he doesn't care and neither do I and once he's fully inside me, he cups the top of my head and thrusts and never takes his eyes off me.

He doesn't kiss me again. He doesn't say a word. He just fucks me hard and deep and maybe this is him reclaiming me. Or claiming me fully for the first time. Making me his. Only his. More so than any brand would have done.

I don't come, and I know that's not the point. But I take him, take his painful thrusts, his weight, his bloodied hand gripping my hair, nails digging into my scalp. I take him and I feel him come, I hear his release and I feel him fill me up and all I can think is I want all of him, all of him. I want to keep him inside me, always. As twisted and wrong as this is, as it's been from day one, I want him.

When he's finished and slides out of me, I feel the warmth of cum on my thigh.

He doesn't move though. He stays on top of me, petting my hair, expression as intense as ever.

"It's done," he says. "It's over. But he deserved better than he got."

He sits up, looks me over once. I sit up too, draw my knees in and hug them.

His gaze settles at my hand and his eyes narrow.

I know what he's looking at.

"Time to bury that, Helena."

I look at the skull ring and he's right. It's past time to bury it. I can't stand having it on my finger anymore. I can't stand the feel of it and I want it off. I need it off.

Sebastian takes my hand and tugs it off and I think I want to scour my skin, scrub away any traces of it, like that will scrub clean the past. Like it will purify it.

Purify us.

He walks out of the room without a word. I watch him go and lay my head against the headboard and think about Gregory, about what he did. And I think I hate myself a little for it.

What happened to him, it's at least partly my

fault. I knew what we were doing, the three of us, it was wrong for him. It hurt him. I knew it would. Inside, I always knew it would.

I don't think he knew that what he demanded of us, that it would break him. I didn't.

But it did.

Last night broke him.

SEBASTIAN

I buried that damned ring.

I put it in the ground where it belongs with the rest of Cain Scafoni.

It's been two weeks since that night. Since Gregory left. I haven't heard anything from him. I've got Gallo looking for him, but I know my brother well enough to know he won't be found until he wants to be.

What he did, I can't get the memory out of my head. Can't stop smelling the smell. Can't stop hearing the sound of his pain.

And I bear the responsibility of it.

It wasn't my intention to hurt him. Sharing Helena was my way of controlling him. I wonder if any of us realized the extent of the damage we were doing all along.

I take a deep breath in, drink a sip of my

steaming coffee and look out over the water, watching the boat approach. The wind is blustery today and the sand like granules of ice under my bare feet.

Amelia Willow is still missing too, which is worrying. A young girl disappearing is different than a man.

I keep tabs on Lucinda, but I'm not worried about her. I control the money which means I control her.

Ethan is still in Philadelphia. Helena's not ready to have him here with us and quite frankly, neither am I.

But she's still not keeping food down and although she was pissed, she's seeing a doctor today.

I swallow the last of my coffee as the boat docks and I climb up to help Dr. price out. Dr. Price was my mother's doctor as well as her friend and she's the one I want tending to Helena.

"Dr. Price, thanks for coming on such short notice," I say, shaking her hand.

"It's no problem, Sebastian."

We talk for a few minutes, her asking about my family, which I lie about, as we make our way to the house.

Helena is still annoyed that I'm insisting on this, but I don't care. She's waiting outside, her eyes betraying her lack of trust.

"Dr. Price, this is Helena. Helena, Dr. Carol Price. She was my mother's doctor."

Helena extends her hand. "Good to meet you, but Sebastian and I are not quite in agreement about me needing a doctor."

"I'm sure he's just being cautious," Dr. Price says. "I promise to make it as easy and painless as possible."

Helena opens her mouth and I go to her, close my hand around the back of her neck and turn her to face me.

"I need you to do this, Helena."

She'll have an examination if I have to hold her down to have it done, but I'm hoping to avoid that route.

"Fine," she says. "But next time, you talk to me before making the arrangements."

"Fine."

I walk them up to my bedroom and as much as I want to stay, I know I should give them privacy, so when my cell phone rings, I excuse myself and go downstairs to the study.

"Hello?" I answer, not recognizing the number, but knowing it's Pennsylvania by the area code.

"Um, hi. Is Helena there?"

It's a girl. And she sounds familiar.

"Who is this?" I ask, but I think I know.

"Her sister. Amelia. Amy."

I sit down. "Where the hell are you, Amelia? Helena's been worried sick."

"I'm sorry about that. I couldn't call until I was settled and sure. I didn't want her to try to send me back."

"Where are you?"

"Philadelphia."

"What are you doing in Philadelphia?"

"Are you going to let her talk to me or are you going to bully me over the phone?"

I chuckle.

"Is this Sebastian?" she asks cautiously. She must have stored my number when Gregory gave Helena my phone to call her that time. I'd made sure he'd used my phone and not his.

"Yes."

She goes quiet.

"Is this your new number, Amelia?"

"Yes."

"Tell me where you are exactly," I say, picking up a pen and finding a blank piece of paper. "I need an address."

She hesitates.

"Don't worry, I'm not getting on a plane to Philadelphia and I won't force you back to the Willow house."

"Okay." She gives me the address of one of the swankiest hotels in the city which immediately sends up flags.

"That's a hotel."

"It's an apartment in the hotel."

"How are you affording that?"

"That's none of your business."

"I just made it my business."

"Look, I just wanted to call to set Helena's mind at ease, not play twenty questions with you. And besides, I have a job."

"A job? Must be a hell of a job to afford that place."

"I'm modeling. I met this man and he thought I had the right look—"

"What man?"

She goes silent.

I wait.

"Is my sister there?" she asks, sounding suddenly years younger than Helena.

"What man, Amelia?"

"No one. Just a new friend I met in the city. It's not like what you're thinking."

"What am I thinking?"

"Can I talk to my sister please?"

"What am I thinking?" I ask again.

No reply.

"I hope you're not doing something stupid, Amelia. If you need money, I'll send some before we get there—"

"I don't want you to come. And I don't need your money. I don't need anything from you but my sister.

Is she locked up somewhere? Is that why I can't talk to her?"

There's a knock on my door and Remy pushes it open. Dr. Price is standing beside him.

"Hold on," I tell Amelia.

"I think you should go upstairs," Dr. Price says.

"Is she okay?"

"She's fine. She's waiting for you."

I nod, stand up. "I'll be right there," I tell the doctor.

She nods and leaves the room.

"Helena's safe and sound. I don't need to keep her locked up. Are you going to be at this number for a little bit?"

"Yes. I'll be here. Look, don't tell her…let me tell her everything, okay?"

"You just stay put, understand?"

"Yes."

I hang up the phone and climb the stairs to Helena's room. She's sitting up in her bed and the color has drained from her face.

I tuck the phone into my pocket and go to her.

"What's going on?"

She looks up at me.

"I'm pregnant."

29

HELENA

"Pregnant?"

Pregnant. To hear the word out loud, it's strange. Foreign.

"How?" he asks.

"How?"

"You had the shot."

"I don't know. I guess I'm that one percent."

"Fuck."

He sits down on the edge of the bed.

I can guess what he's thinking. I'm thinking the same thing.

"They can do a paternity test in a few weeks."

Sebastian nods.

I cover my face, take a deep breath, exhale.

"Can we talk about something else? Please? I can't do this right now. I have to wrap my brain around it."

"Yeah." He looks at me. "We can talk about your sister."

"Amy?"

"That was her calling."

"How did she get your phone number?"

"It's the phone you used to call her. That wasn't Gregory's. It was mine."

"How…is she okay?"

"She sounds fine." He reaches into his pocket to retrieve his phone. "Here. Call her back. I saved the number. I'm going to go get some air."

I nod, take the phone and watch him go, then call the number back and a moment later, Amy's on the line and I'm too relieved to be angry. I don't tell her my news but that's only because I'm having a hard time believing it myself just yet. And I need to make sure she's okay.

She's apparently in Philadelphia. Sebastian has the address. And she's found a job with a modeling agency.

"But how did you get an apartment? A phone? You need money for those things."

"Oh, the agency fronted it," she says, but she says it too quickly, almost tripping over the words and I think she's lying.

"Amy?"

"Look, I have to go. It's okay, Helena. I'm fine. I have everything under control."

"Are you sure? This whole thing seems too good

to be true. I mean, the apartment, a phone, and clothes?"

"Yes, I'm sure. I'll be working to earn it back. But, are you okay? Sebastian sounds really bossy, Helena."

"Bossy?" I almost laugh.

"Yeah. I only talked to him for like two minutes and I can tell."

"Bossy is an understatement. But he's fine. Things are...different now." I put a hand on my belly.

"You sound different than the last time. Better."

"I am better."

"Do you think he'll let you come visit me?"

"I think I can convince him we need to take a trip to Philadelphia. Have you talked to mom and dad? Told them where you are?"

"I don't want to talk to them. They're not just going to let me go."

"You're twenty-one years old. You're an adult. It's not up to them."

"You know how they are."

"Yeah, I know. Maybe at least send some word that you're safe."

"Like they care about our safety."

"Just do it, okay?" Sometimes I feel like a big sister, like I'm years older than her. It's always been that way with us.

"Have you called them, Helena? Told them off? Told them to go to hell for what they did to you?"

"No."

"Do you hate them?"

"No. I don't know. Things turned out differently than I thought they would. Sebastian…I love him."

"Helena!"

"I know. It's crazy. But, well, all of this has been crazy."

"You're in love. With him. A Scafoni. Oh my God."

"I'm worried about you, Amy."

"I know and I'm sorry for making you worry, but I need to do this my way. I need to come to terms with everything. Okay?"

I nod, even though she can't see me. "Okay. I understand."

"Thanks, Helena. You can call me anytime now, okay?"

"I will and same. Take care and I love you, sis." I feel tears warm my eyes.

"I love you. And you be careful."

We hang up the phone and I go into the bathroom and wash my face. I look at myself in the mirror, lift my shirt a little to look at my belly. It's still flat, but it's early. Just four to six weeks, the doctor though. My breasts are already a little fuller and tender. I hadn't even noticed. But then again, there has been a lot going on.

I'm not ready to have a baby.

I'm not ready to have one with him.

And then there's the other thing.

What if it's not his?

What if it's Gregory's?

30

SEBASTIAN

The next few weeks are tense. Helena is still having trouble keeping food down and the stress of it all is weighing on her.

Hell, it's sitting on me like a ton of bricks.

A baby.

She's fucking pregnant.

This wasn't supposed to happen. This isn't part of the plan.

Although what is the plan? What the hell has it ever been?

Take the Willow Girl.

Break her.

That was the plan.

Destroy a life like we Scafoni men do.

Destroy our own in the process.

I wasn't ever supposed to fall in love with her.

I don't even know when it happened. How it

happened. But I did fall in love, and now, she's carrying my baby.

Or my brother's baby.

What the hell are we going to do if it's his? What will she want to do?

I just can't think about it yet. Not until we get the results of the paternity test which will be today. They took blood from Helena and swabbed my cheek earlier in the week. Dr. Price received the results of the test this morning.

Helena's been quieter than normal, and we haven't talked about what we're going to do. I don't have a clue what she's thinking or where her head is.

When we arrive, the nurse takes us into the doctor's office right away. I don't know what Dr. Price thinks about this paternity test and quite frankly, could give a fuck, but once we're settled, she opens a folder and takes out the envelope that holds the results. She smiles at us a little awkwardly and I realize I'm sitting on the edge of my seat when Helena slides her hand across to touch me.

We exchange a look and I slip her hand between mine as the doctor adjusts her glasses and reads the results.

"Well?" I ask anxiously.

She smiles, turns it over and pushes it toward us.

"You're the father, Sebastian."

Helena lets out an audible exhale.

I turn to her, smile, not realizing how tense I've been. And I'm surprised at the excitement I feel.

"Now, Helena, your blood also showed higher than usual levels of hCG—"

"What's that?" I ask. "Is that a problem?"

"A hormone produced during pregnancy, and no, not a problem," she replies with a smile. She turns back to Helena. "Given the history of multiples in your family, I'd feel better if we did an Ultrasound."

"Multiples?" Helena asks, sounding lost.

"It could be nothing. Some women have higher levels of this hormone and they carry a single child. We'd need to do the Ultrasound to be sure."

Helena's lost a little color.

I turn to the doctor.

"Why don't you give us a few minutes," I say.

The doctor nods and vacates the room.

A tear slides from Helena's eye and she wipes it away.

"Why are you crying?"

"I'm relieved it's yours but..."

"Are you happy?"

She looks at me. "It's really fast. Not normal."

"Yeah. Well, what's been normal about any of this?"

"Nothing." She looks at her lap and worry creases her brow.

"Helena?"

She shifts her gaze up at mine. "I'm not ready for this."

I feel my jaw tense. "We can talk about it."

"What if...what if it's four? Four girls?"

I wipe the tears off her face with my thumbs and lift her onto my lap.

"What if it's already happening again?" she asks into my chest. "The cycle starting already."

"It's not. It's over."

She gives a small shake of her head.

"It's over, Helena. There won't be another Willow Girl reaping." I tilt her face up so she looks at me. "I swear it. This is us finishing it. With this birth, whether it's one or four, it's finished. The Willow Girl Legacy, it's over. And what has it done over centuries? Destroyed both families. Turned brother against brother. Daughter against mother. And caused too much pain and suffering."

She rests her head against my chest and touches my face with her fingertips.

"The families will be united again, but this time, it'll be out of love, not greed," I say. "I love you and I'll have one baby with you or four babies or a dozen. I don't care. I love you. And whatever this is, we're doing it together, you and me."

She nods.

"Ready?"

Her smile wavers but I stand her up and squeeze her arms. I'll be strong enough for both of us.

"Doctor," I call out.

Dr. Price re-enters and a few moments later, Helena is lying on the table and we're all staring into the monitor and hearing the echo, a whooshing sound, as the doctor finds the baby.

The babies.

All four of them.

EPILOGUE 1

HELENA

One Month Later

Sebastian is right. My aunt Helena was right.
We're ending this, he and I.
I'll be the last Willow Girl.

We're sitting in Joseph Gallo's office as he talks through the contract on his desk. It's a new one Sebastian had drawn up that signs over the deed of the Willow estate and land to me. It also marks a symbolic end of the taking of the Willow Girls.

I talked to my parents a few days after the doctor's visit. I didn't tell them about the pregnancy. I didn't tell them about Sebastian and me. After my conversation with Amy, when she asked me if I hated them, I couldn't get the question out of my head.

They know the house is being transferred to my name. They also know I plan on demolishing it before I sell the land.

It's the house Marius Willow took his bride, Anabelle Scafoni. It's where all of this began. And I'm ending it.

Once the land is sold, I'll give them the money, split it between my parents and sisters because I don't want a penny of it. I don't want anything to do with it or with them because I am angry. I'm angry at all of them.

My parents sold me. They would have sold any of us. And my sisters lived off that money. I can't forgive them, not yet. Maybe not ever.

But I don't think I hate them.

Sebastian offers to destroy the heavy tome that contains the records of the Willow Girls, but I take it, instead. I want to keep it. A Willow should keep it. Should remember them because they were cast aside by their families too. Sold. Their lives destroyed.

And having it under my arm as we walk out of that building, it's like a sisterhood almost. And it's right. As right as that bone-ring was wrong.

"Lunch?" Sebastian asks.

"I'm starving," I say. It seems I'm always starving ever since I found out I was pregnant.

Pregnant with quadruplets.

We can find out the sex of the babies in a few more months, but I already know. I think he does too. We'll have four girls.

He takes my hand and we walk to the same restaurant we came to the last time we were here. And we take the same table except that today, we appear to be the only customers. Once he has a glass of wine and I sparkling water, he leans in toward me.

"How are you feeling about things? The babies?"

"What do you mean?"

"Do you want to keep them?"

I look at him. "That's never been a question for me."

"Good. I feel the same way." He sips from his wine then reaches into his pocket and takes out a small, black-velvet box and sets it on the table between us.

I look at it and it takes my brain a minute to process even though my heart knows.

"What are you doing?" I ask him as he opens the box.

I turn my gaze up to his and he's smiling but it's a different sort of smile than I usually see on him. This one, it's happy and a little unsure, maybe.

"In the short time I've known you, you have gotten under my skin, Helena Willow. You have turned my life upside-down, and I'm...happy. In spite of all the crap we've been through, I'm happy. I don't know if I deserve to be, but I am. I love you and I want to marry you. So, this is me telling you I plan to keep you forever. Marry me, Helena."

"Sebastian—"

"Now. Marry me now."

EPILOGUE 2

SEBASTIAN

"What if I'd said no?" she asks as I lead her up to my room—our room—once we're back on the island after the civil ceremony. I'd arranged for the ceremony before we went to Gallo's office to sign that paperwork and not once did it occur to me she might say no.

"You weren't going to."

"You're arrogant, Sebastian Scafoni."

"And you're beautiful, Mrs. Scafoni."

I lift her up in my arms when I push the door open and carry her inside, kicking the door closed and setting her on her feet beside the bed.

"Besides, I'm old fashioned when it comes to bringing babies into the world. I want us married first," I say.

"I still think you're arrogant to assume I'd say yes."

"You did say yes."

I kiss her, unzipping the back of her dress as I do, peeling it off her shoulders and letting it drop to the floor. I stand back and look at her. Her breasts are swollen to twice their size, giving me a good handful, and although she says she sees a bump, I see the tiniest swell. Maybe.

"You're fucking beautiful, you know that?" I say.

"I'm going to get fat."

"I hope so. Fat with my babies. And about that. I lied earlier. It does matter. I want dozens. Dozens of boys and girls to run around here and bring joy back to this island. This house."

She giggles as I peel off her bra. She reaches for the hem of my sweater and pulls it over my head.

I wrap one arm around her and pull her in, kissing her as I slide the other into her panties and cup her wet pussy. I draw back, look at her as I run my fingers over one breast before turning her, pushing her onto her hands and knees on the bed and peeling her panties down to mid-thigh.

Splaying her open, I feel ravenous suddenly and dip my head to feast on her pussy, tasting her, licking the arousal from her before wrapping a hand in her hair and drawing her to stand to kiss her mouth again, my mouth sticky with her.

Her fingertips play across the muscles of my belly, then dip lower, undoing my jeans. She slides her hand inside and looks up at me.

"I want to taste you, Sebastian."

Fuck.

Yes.

I twist my hand in her hair and push her to her knees. She undoes my jeans the rest of the way and pushes them down and I watch her take me, watch her on her knees swallowing me into her mouth and I know it's going to take all I have not to blow down her throat.

The light bounces off the diamond ring on its platinum band on her finger and I smile, pushing her backward until her head is resting against the bed, leaning into her, watching her face, her eyes, as she takes me, as I fuck her face.

My wife.

She's my wife now.

I let out a moan and pull out, draw her to stand, and when I kiss her, I taste myself on her lips.

I lay her on the bed and, still standing, I slide into her dripping pussy.

"Fuck. You're always so wet for me."

I watch as she stretches to take me, the wet sounds of her pussy making me harder. I won't last long and I pull out, turn her over. I draw her ass cheeks apart and slide into her from behind, my thumb on her asshole, rubbing it, hearing how she moans when I do that.

I lean over her, grip her hands, intertwine our fingers, feel my ring on her left hand.

"You're all mine, Helena. Forever" I say, my mouth to her ear, her cheek. "All mine."

"I was always yours, Sebastian," she says, her voice hitching as she kisses me. "Always."

The End

Keep reading for a sample from TWISTED, Gregory Scafoni's story!

EXCERPT FROM TWISTED

Prologue
Amelia

He says that together they twisted him.

Made him the monster he's become.

But you can't become something that wasn't inside you all along.

A tear drops to the sketchbook on my lap, the blob smearing the lead. I wipe it away with the tip of my finger and watch the stain spread to the edge of the page.

I can't seem to stop drawing that night.

The night when the Scafoni brothers stalked into our home and we were made to wear those rotting, disgusting sheaths and forced to stand on those ancient blocks as Sebastian Scafoni, first-born bastard, looked us over like we were cattle.

I can't stop drawing the look on his face when he saw Helena.

Even if she wasn't bound like she was, she'd have stood out.

She always thought herself the ugly duckling but she's the most beautiful of all. She's special. Always was. Different from us. And so much stronger.

Crap.

I swipe the back of my hand across my nose and listen to the sound of tears drop fat and heavy onto the page and this time when I lay my hand on the sketch, it's to smear the wet across like maybe I can wipe away that night. Rub it off the page. Erase it out of history like it never happened.

"Oh, now look what you've done," he says. His voice is deep and low, and I swear I can feel it as much as hear it.

He takes my hand with his gloved one and pulls it away.

"Ruined it."

I look at him. I finally make myself look at him.

"I hate you."

He grins. Shrugs a shoulder, his grip growing infinitesimally harder.

I glance at my palm—it's black from the pencil—and look down at the page in front of me.

He's right. It's ruined.

But it doesn't matter. I have dozens like it.

Hundreds.

Thousands.

I can't stop drawing that night.

Can't stop it from happening.

Can't stop the Scafoni bastards from walking into our lives, upending everything. Coming into our home like kings, like they owned the place.

Although, I guess they did.

They owned everything. Our house. Our land. Our parents.

My sister.

Me.

I force myself to meet Gregory Scafoni's dark eyes with their strange turquoise specks and wonder how I'd ever thought he was an angel.

My angel.

My savior.

When all he is, is the devil.

Buy Now!

THANK YOU

Thank you for reading *Torn!* I hope you enjoyed this final part of Sebastian and Helena's story. If you'd consider leaving a review at the store where you purchased this book, I would be so very grateful.

Make sure to sign up for my newsletter to stay updated on news and giveaways! You can find the link on my website: https://natasha-knight.com/subscribe/

Like my FB Author Page to keep updated on news and giveaways!

I have a FB Fan Group where I share exclusive teasers, giveaways and just fun stuff. Probably TMI :) It's called The Knight Spot. I'd love for you to join us!

ALSO BY NATASHA KNIGHT

Collateral Damage Duet

Collateral: an Arranged Marriage Mafia Romance
Damage: an Arranged Marriage Mafia Romance

Ties that Bind Duet

Mine

His

Dark Legacy Trilogy

Taken (Dark Legacy, Book 1)
Torn (Dark Legacy, Book 2)
Twisted (Dark Legacy, Book 3)

MacLeod Brothers

Devil's Bargain

Benedetti Mafia World

Salvatore: a Dark Mafia Romance
Dominic: a Dark Mafia Romance

Sergio: a Dark Mafia Romance

The Benedetti Brothers Box Set (Contains Salvatore, Dominic and Sergio)

Killian: a Dark Mafia Romance

Giovanni: a Dark Mafia Romance

The Amado Brothers

Dishonorable

Disgraced

Unhinged

Standalone Dark Romance

Descent

Deviant

Beautiful Liar

Retribution

Theirs To Take

Captive, Mine

Alpha

Given to the Savage

Taken by the Beast

Claimed by the Beast

Captive's Desire

Protective Custody

Amy's Strict Doctor

Taming Emma

Taming Megan

Taming Naia

Reclaiming Sophie

The Firefighter's Girl

Dangerous Defiance

Her Rogue Knight

Taught To Kneel

Tamed: the Roark Brothers Trilogy

ACKNOWLEDGMENTS

Cover Design by CoverLuv

Editing by Casey McKay

ABOUT THE AUTHOR

USA Today bestselling author of contemporary romance, Natasha Knight specializes in dark, tortured heroes. Happily-Ever-Afters are guaranteed, but she likes to put her characters through hell to get them there. She's evil like that.

Want more?
www.natasha-knight.com
natasha-knight@outlook.com